WATTS WRITERS WORKSHOP

Written by

Darryl Harvey

Loosely based on, Budd Schulberg and The Watts Writers Workshop

94th Place Films
L.A, CA 90047

INT. HOME OF BUDD SCHULBERG - LIVING ROOM - DAY

A framed poster of the film *On the Waterfront* hangs on the
wall as the voice of a NEWS REPORTER is heard.

                    NEWS REPORTER (V.O.)
          The afternoon fires have added to
          the chaos that is now Southeast Los
          Angeles...

A framed black and white photo of Budd Schulberg with Marlon
Brando, and Karl Malden hangs on the wall.

Again, the voice of a News Reporter is heard.

                    NEWS REPORTER (V.O.)
          ...Riots which had quieted down
          during the dawn sprang again into
          full-scale violence this morning...

On the wall hangs another framed black and white photo of
four gentlemen wearing tuxedos, each holding Oscars, it's
Budd Schulberg standing with Elia Kazan, Boris Kaufman, and
Richard Day.

Once again the voice of a News Reporter is heard.

                    NEWS REPORTER (V.O.)
          ...New rioting flared in the
          Southeast area. Angry mobs of
          Negro youths and adults moved
          through their sealed-off area...

Displayed on the mantle are numerous awards with the name
Budd Schulberg inscribed on them. One statuette that
prominently stands out, is an OSCAR. The gold plate affixed
on the Oscar reads, *Budd Schulberg best screenplay.*

And again, the voice of a News Reporter is heard.

                    NEWS REPORTER (V.O.)
          ...Behind them a trail of blood.
          Literally, hundreds of cars were
          overturned and wrecked. Key things
          that were taken were about a
          hundred firearms with ammunition.
          Cars by the dozen were burned, the
          occupants were pulled out and
          beaten.

Standing in front of the television set with a troubled
facial expression and rubbing his chin is BUDD SCHULBERG, a
51-year-old white male.

Images of L.A.P.D. Officers wearing riot helmets wielding nightsticks, chasing down Negroes, arresting and beating them flash across the television screen.

GERALDINE BROOKS an attractive 30-year-old white female walks up and stands next to Budd. Geraldine has a vexed look as she stares at the television.

> GERALDINE
> Budd, this is scary. The rioting
> could spread across L.A. What if
> it reaches us?

> BUDD
> (slight stammer)
> I don't think so. The governor has
> called in the National Guard.

> GERALDINE
> The Negroes are destroying their
> own community. What could that
> possibly accomplish?

> BUDD
> Watts was a powder keg of
> frustration, and now it's exploded.

> GERALDINE
> Maybe Martin Luther King can help?

> BUDD
> Maybe. It's apparent the blacks of
> Watts embraced the speeches of
> Malcolm X and the Black Panther
> Party. Violence is the only
> solution.

More images flash across the television screen of blacks rioting, looting, and buildings set ablaze, police wielding nightsticks, shoving and clubbing Negroes. The voice of a News Reporter is heard.

> NEWS REPORTER (V.O.)
> Molotov cocktails have been flying
> through the air causing
> destruction. Rioters attacked
> whites and Negroes alike. One
> hundred forty-eight arrests for
> theft, shooting, and throwing
> missiles. And this is almost
> unbelievable in view of all this...

> BUDD
> Geraldine, I have to do something.

                    GERALDINE
          Budd don't even think about it.
          Don't you go down there?

                    BUDD
          That uprising parallels my novel
          "Day of the Locust." The
          protagonist whose masterpiece was a
          painting titled *"The Burning of Los
          Angeles."*

                    GERALDINE
          -- Uprising? You're a Hollywood
          writer, not a black militant.

                    BUDD
          I need to go down there and see for
          myself.

                    GERALDINE
          The last thing those Negroes want
          to see is some empathetic white
          man. You'll get yourself killed.

INT. CAR - DAY

MUSIC CUE: "Ole Man Trouble" by Otis Redding.

Budd slowly drives and surveys the charred remains of the
burnt-up buildings.

Negroes mill about, some look lost. Budd catches eye contact
with some of the Negroes and they don't look too happy to see
his presents.

END MUSIC CUE:

The voice of radio personality MAGNIFICENT MONTAGUE comes
over the airwaves...

                    MAGNIFICENT MONTAGUE (V.O.)
          "Burn, baby, burn!" That was Otis
          Redding, *"Ole Man Trouble."* You're
          listening to Magnificent Montague,
          and it's the calm after the
          storm...

Budd lowers the volume on the radio. As he continues to
cruise, Budd notices a pale-green two-story stucco building
that hasn't been touched by the fires, it stood alone
completely undamaged. Painted on the window in big block
letters reads, *Westminster Neighborhood Assn. Inc.*

Budd pulls over to the curb and parks. He gets out and walks into the Westminster Neighborhood Association building.

INT. WESTMINSTER NEIGHBORHOOD ASSOCIATION - LOBBY - DAY

ARCHIE HARDWICK an African American in his 30s is interacting with several black youths. The guys are wearing slim-fit trousers, button-down shirts, loafers, Fedora hats, and dark shades. The girls are wearing cigarette pants, pencil skirts, and open and closed-toe flats.

When Budd walks in he draws all the attention and is greeted with very suspicious looks -- Archie with a no-nonsense look, breaks the ice...

                    ARCHIE
          What can I do for you?

                    BUDD
          I saw the sign on the window.

                    ARCHIE
          Uh-huh.

                    BUDD
          Well, I was curious about what goes
          on here.

                    ARCHIE
          I'm not sure what you mean.

The group of black youths gives Budd a stern look. Budd looks uncomfortable and somewhat nervous.

                    BUDD
          May I speak with you for a moment?

Archie turns to the group of black youths.

                    ARCHIE
          Look, ah, give me a minute. Let me
          talk to this guy.

Some of the black youths go upstairs, while others exit the front door.

Archie approaches Budd.

                    ARCHIE (CONT'D)
          What do you want mister?

                    BUDD
I'm Budd Schulberg. After watching
the riots unfold on TV, I felt
compelled to come to Watts. I want
to help in any way I can.

                    ARCHIE
Guilt complex?

                    BUDD
If that's what you want to call it.
I just know I have a deep desire to
help the people of Watts.

                    ARCHIE
You sound sincere.

                    BUDD
Oh, I am.

                    ARCHIE
What is it that you want to do? I
mean, how can you help?

                    BUDD
I'm only one man, but I want to
start a writing class.

                    ARCHIE
     (scratching head)
A writing class?

                    BUDD
Yes.

                    ARCHIE
I guess you didn't notice all the
burnt-down buildings? I don't see
how a writing class can help with
reconstruction, or finding jobs for
that matter.

                    BUDD
Writing has a number of benefits.
There is a direct correlation
between writing and productivity.
I'm sorry what's your name?

                    ARCHIE
Archie, Archie Hardwick. Look Mr.
Schulberg...

                    BUDD
...Please, call me Budd.

                         ARCHIE
          Budd. -- It's no accident that
          this building was spared during the
          riots. The Westminster
          Neighborhood Association is the
          largest private social-service
          agency in Watts. I'm constantly in
          the streets attempting to reason
          with rioters.

                         BUDD
          We have the same mindset, just a
          different approach. Given the
          chance. I think I can effect
          change.

                         ARCHIE
          This is a space for residents of
          all faiths to converge and
          organize. We host youth clubs and
          civic organizations, collaborating
          with non-church groups to address
          the neighborhood's impoverishment.

                         BUDD
          Then I'm in the right place.

                         ARCHIE
          There is a different type of Negro
          emerging from ages eighteen to
          twenty-five... they identify with
          Malcolm X's philosophy. You'll be
          seen as an outsider. Watts may not
          be the safest place for you.

                         BUDD
          My wife said the same thing.

                         ARCHIE
          Maybe you should listen to your
          wife.

                         BUDD
          Are you trying to discourage me?

Archie takes a thumb tack and posts a *notice* on the bulletin
board, it reads, *Creative Writing Class every Wednesday at 3
PM, all interested sign below.*

Archie turns and looks at Budd.

                         ARCHIE
          Good luck.

INT. HOME OF BUDD SCHULBERG - DINING ROOM - EVENING

Budd and Geraldine are seated at the table having a meal.

                    GERALDINE
          I just don't think it's a good
          idea. Not because I don't want you
          to help the Negroes in Watts. I'm
          concerned for your safety.

                    BUDD
          Who knows where this will go? I
          can use my influence to shift
          thinking. Expressive culture
          through writing, is an alternative
          for frustrated black youths who
          would otherwise be susceptible to
          militant appeals.

                    GERALDINE
          So you're an activist now?

                    BUDD
          I've always been an activist.

                    GERALDINE
          Oh, God.

                    BUDD
          Look, if it doesn't work. At least
          I tried.

INT. WESTMINSTER NEIGHBORHOOD ASSOCIATION - ROOM - DAY

Sitting alone, surrounded by clutter, Budd shuffles through
notes and idly reads the community paper.

BLACK YOUTH #1 and BLACK YOUTH #2 wearing slim-fit trousers,
button-down shirts, and loafers walk in. They pause and
check Budd out as if he's some sort of oddity.

                    BUDD
          Hello. Are you here for the
          writing class?

Black Youth #1 and Black Youth #2 glower at Budd.

                    BLACK YOUTH #1
          You ain't welcome here honky.

Budd stands up from the chair and walks up to Black Youth #1
and Black Youth #2.

                         BUDD
          Why don't you give it a chance?
          Express your feelings in writing.

Black Youth #2 scowl on his face and a toothpick in his
mouth.

                    BLACK YOUTH #2
          You best go back to where you came
          from. Understand.

Black Youth #1 and Black Youth #2 walk out, leaving Budd
looking frustrated.

INT. WESTMINSTER NEIGHBORHOOD ASSOCIATION - LOBBY - LATER

Archie is standing with SAMUEL HARRIS an African American
male age 16. It appears the two are talking when Budd walks
up.

                         BUDD
          Hey, Archie, I'm going to take off.
          I'll give it another try next week.

                        ARCHIE
          Ok -- Hey, um, ah -- I want you
          to meet Samuel. Sam, this is Budd
          Schulberg, he runs the writing
          class.

Samuel acknowledges Budd with a slight head nod.

                         BUDD
          Well, it's not much of a class.
          I've been coming for weeks and no
          one has shown up. Samuel, maybe
          you'd like to attend the class.

                        SAMUEL
          Maybe. I saw the notice on the
          bulletin board. Looks like some
          potential students left you a
          message, go check it out.

Budd walks over to the bulletin board. Scrawled on the
notice is, "Take your writing class and shove it up your
ass."

EXT. WATTS - 103RD & BEACH STREET - DAY

Burnt-out buildings obtrude as Budd aimlessly wanders, the
mutterings of disenchanted Negroes don't go unnoticed.

Standing a few yards from Budd is NEGRO RESIDENT #1.

                    NEGRO RESIDENT #1
          Dig the gray beast!

Looking pissed off, NEGRO RESIDENT #2 stands next to Negro
Resident #1.

                    NEGRO RESIDENT #2
          What the fug you think he's up to?

A lean, RAGGED YOUNGSTER who looks and sounds like a teen-age
Malcolm X challenges Budd as he passes by.

                    RAGGED YOUNGSTER
          The white man's heaven is the black
          man's hell!

INT. HOME OF JOHNIE SCOTT - NEXT DAY

There's a knock at the door. JOHNIE SCOTT African American
male 19, walks up to the door.

                    JOHNIE
          Who is it?

                    SAMUEL (O.C.)
          It's me man, Samuel.

Johnie opens the door and Samuel walks in.

                    SAMUEL (CONT'D)
          Ay, man, I was at Westminster
          yesterday, and some white cat was
          up there hanging out.

                    JOHNIE
          Oh, yeah, was he trying to make
          trouble?

                    SAMUEL
          I don't know. Archie said the
          cat's name is Schulberg.

                    JOHNIE
          Schulberg?

                    SAMUEL
          Yeah. The dude is trying to start
          a writer's group. Asked me if I
          wanted to check it out.

                    JOHNIE
Huh?

                    SAMUEL
A lot of the brotha's don't want
him down there. They're suspicious
of that cat.

                    JOHNIE
I'd be too. A white man hanging
out in Watts right after the riots.

                    SAMUEL
Johnie, man, I want you to check
the dude out. See if he's for
real.

                    JOHNIE
Me? Why, me?

                    SAMUEL
Yeah, you ah college dude, Harvard
and all. You probably can relate
to that cat.

                    JOHNIE
Ex-Harvard dude. I dropped out,
remember? Man, I don't know. If
Archie trusts him...

                    SAMUEL
...That's just it. He might be
trying to hustle the community.

Johnie takes a deep breath and rubs his chin.

EXT. BEVERLY HILLS CAFÉ - DAY

Sitting at a quaint little table is ADELINE SCHULBERG, a 77-
year-old vibrant silver hair white woman wearing a formal
black sweater with a white fur Ermine collar, and earrings.

Sitting across from Adeline is Budd, dressed in his usual
drab casual attire.

                    ADELINE
Budd, I have a few things lined up
for you. So, look...

                    BUDD
...Adeline, I can't take on
anything right now.

                    ADELINE
          Don't call me that, call me Mom.
          And what do you mean you can't take
          on anything right now? Paramount
          has an untitled Bob Hope project.
          They want you to write the script,
          it pays one hundred thousand.

                    BUDD
          I'm sorry Mom, but I'm committed to
          the writer's class in Watts. I'm
          sorry.

                    ADELINE
          Your sorry, I'm sorry. I'm your
          agent, we need each other, that's
          how the bills get paid.

                    BUDD
          There is talent in Watts. I want
          to nurture that talent and help it
          flourish.

                    ADELINE
          Can't you just make a donation to
          there cause? Find someone to take
          over the class.

                    BUDD
          No, I'm not going to do that.

                    ADELINE
          Turning down jobs in Hollywood,
          especially from powerful executives
          is not a good look son.

                    BUDD
          Mother, this going to be an onerous
          journey that will take up the
          majority of my time.

                    ADELINE
          Mother?
               (perturbed)
          Babysitting a bunch of Negroes in
          Watts -- argh.

INT. WESTMINSTER NEIGHBORHOOD ASSOCIATION - ROOM - DAY

Johnie Scott sits among a group of highly charged youthful
Negroes. Almost in unison, their dissenting voices erupt. A
rough-looking surly 18-year-old NEGRO #1, juts up from a
chair.

                         NEGRO #1
             I was on a motherfuckin' chain gang
             in the South. Every goddam day the
             man takes me out and beats my ass.
             Finally I get away and hitchhike to
             L.A. New Scene. Another chance.
             Two days later I'm busted here.
             Not doin' nothin', jus' huntin' me
             a place to sleep. The man picks me
             up and whops on me jus' like back
             home. Shi-it, man, I had it with
             whitey.

An articulate 20-year-old, NEGRO #2 stands up from their
chair.

                         NEGRO #2
             The problem is the standard for
             discussion is set by the whites and
             a lot of Negroes don't want to
             accept that standard anymore, they
             wanna, ah, they say, "We gonna have
             our own standard." I think that
             the hookup comes if you can develop
             a whole new standard where whites
             and Negroes can have a dialogue,
             not either one of those are
             acceptable anymore. I mean whites
             aren't gonna accept Negro standards
             and Negroes no longer wanna be
             white, so the clear thing is to
             develop a whole new standard and
             then everybody move toward that, so
             there can be some sort of dialogue.

NEGRO #3 chimes in...

                         NEGRO #3
             Black people are being brainwashed
             into thinking in order for us to
             exist, we must resort to using hair
             straighteners so our hair won't be
             kinky, that if we could only hide
             our blackness, we can then become
             part of this thing called the
             American dream.

The disgruntled Negroes caterwaul, their griping becomes
deafening. Budd stands in front of the crowd of Negroes, he
looks a bit frazzled.

Johnie Scott steps out from among the group and stands next
to Budd. Johnie waves his arms getting the attention of the
Negroes.

                         JOHNIE
              Alright, calm down. Calm down,
              please!

The Negroes begin to settle down, and the clamoring has
ceased. Among them is passive observer 19-year-old CHARLES
JOHNSON, African American.

                         JOHNIE (CONT'D)
              Let's give this man a break. If he
              comes back after this, then we'll
              know if he's for real or not.

EXT. WESTMINSTER NEIGHBORHOOD ASSOCIATION - SIDEWALK - LATER

Some Negro teens are hanging out front smoking cigarettes,
and talking.

Johnie walks out front followed by Budd. They stand a few
yards away from the Negro teens.

                         BUDD
                    (slight stammer)
              Thanks for coming to my rescue. It
              was pretty tense in there.

                         JOHNIE
              I guess I'm gonna have to mediate
              for you from now on. -- Johnie
              Scott.

Johnie extends his hand. Budd doesn't hesitate, he shakes
Johnie's hand.

                         BUDD
              Budd...

                         JOHNIE
              ...Schulberg. I know.

                         BUDD
              Word travels fast around here.

                         JOHNIE
              Yeah, we have our ways of getting
              the word out.

                         BUDD
              So, were you interested in the
              writing class? Or were you just
              checking me out?

                    JOHNIE
          A little of both.

Charles Johnson comes out front and walks up to Budd.

                    CHARLES
          That was a highly charged
          atmosphere. Equal to that of the
          riot.

                    JOHNIE
          I don't think so, or he wouldn't
          have come out alive.

                    BUDD
          Charles, this is Johnie.

                    JOHNIE
          What's happen'en man?

                    CHARLES
          I've seen you around.

                    JOHNIE
          I'm cool with Archie. I come by
          every now and then.

                    BUDD
          Charles is the workshop's first
          serious participant.

                    CHARLES
          Well, I gotta run. I'll see you
          next week Budd. I'll catch you
          later Johnie.

                    JOHNIE
          Later, man.

Charles walks off.

                    BUDD
               (turns to Johnie)
          Have you signed up?

                    JOHNIE
          Not yet.

                    BUDD
          The writing class is...

                    JOHNIE
          ...Every Wednesday at three PM.

                         BUDD
          I guess I'll see you then?

                         JOHNIE
          Yeah. Yeah, you will.

INT. HOME OF BUDD SCHULBERG - OFFICE - EVENING

Budd turns on a lamp and sits down at his desk. He goes
threw his Rolodex.

Budd picks up his phone and begins to dial.

                         BUDD
          -- Hello, Jimmy, this is Budd. --
          I'm fine -- yeah, right. I
          started a writing class. -- Uh,
          huh -- I'm teaching Negroes. I'm
          going to need your support. --
          It's at the Westminster
          Neighborhood Association in Watts.
          -- Whatever you can contribute. --
          That's right, one hundred and third
          street. They call it Charcoal
          Alley. -- Great, I will. -- OK,
          bye.

As Budd hangs up the phone, he looks up and Geraldine walks
in with a food tray.

                         GERALDINE
          You need to slow down and eat.

Geraldine sits the food in front of Budd.

                         BUDD
          Looks good.

Budd picks up a fork and takes a few bites of food.

                         GERALDINE
          Who were you talking to?

                         BUDD
          Jimmy. He said to tell you hi. I
          asked him to support the class

                         GERALDINE
          What'd he say?

                         BUDD
          Sure. Whatever he could do.

Budd takes another bite of food.

                    GERALDINE
          Well, that's good. Who else are
          you going to call?

                    BUDD
          Whomever I think will listen.

EXT. STUDIO WATTS - 103RD & GRANDEE AVENUE - DAY

ERIC PRIESTLY African American male 21 walks in from off the
street.

INT. STUDIO WATTS - CONTINUOUS

In a large spacious area, Negroes are separated into groups.

Some Negroes stand at easels painting, other Negroes are
engaged in modern African dance steps, and still other
Negroes mold and sculpt clay that sits atop a sculpting
wheel.

Youthful-looking Negroes sit in a semi-circle as JAYNE CORTEZ
African American female 31, rhythmically recites poetry to
the beat of a jazz drummer.

                    JAYNE
               (hip cool)
          The slash of a barracuda is not
          like the gulp of a leaping whale.
          The speech of a tiger shark is not
          like the bark of a eagle fish. The
          sent of a gardenia is not like the
          scent of a tangerine --
               (croon)
          Find your own voice and use it.
          Use your own voice and find it.
          Find your own voice and use it.
          Use your own voice and find it.
          Find it, find it, find it, find it,
          find it...

The Youthful-looking Negroes in the semi-circle applaud. At
the same time, Eric walks up clapping his hands.

                    JAYNE (CONT'D)
          Syncopation. "A disturbance or
          interruption of the regular flow of
          rhythm." Express that in your
          writing. It may sound a little
          off, dig deep down inside of you.
               (MORE)

>   JAYNE (CONT'D)
>   Poetry has its own rhythm, let it
>   flow unto the page.

Just then JAMES WOODS an African American male in his late
30s walks in.

>   JAMES
>   Can I have everyone's attention
>   please, gather round.

All of the Negroes huddle together around James.

>   JAMES (CONT'D)
>   I want to address the new students,
>   you regular students know me. I'm
>   James Wood director and
>   administrator of Studio Watts. In
>   order to work in this space,
>   artists must agree to give public
>   exhibitions of their work at least
>   two times a year in Watts and in an
>   artistic space outside the area,
>   and also to provide free
>   instruction to any student with,
>   "the initiative and the desire to
>   participate in the creative arts."
>   Most of you know Jayne Cortez, for
>   those that don't, she is the
>   director of the acting and writing
>   program. With that said, "Do your
>   thang."

Eric pulls Jayne to the side.

>   ERIC
>   Jayne, I'm gonna check out a new
>   writing class at Westminster.

>   JAYNE
>   You talken' bout that dude up the
>   street? You're not leaving us, are
>   you?

>   ERIC
>   Ah, naw. I just wanted to know
>   what you think.

>   JAYNE
>   Eric, you're free to come and go
>   brotha. The door is always open
>   here.

>   ERIC
>   Cool, thanks.

INT. MOVIE STUDIO SET - DAY

Under the bright lights, a film crew is at work.

Two actors are on stage performing an intimate kissing scene.

A camera operator is behind the camera. A boom operator
man's the sound dolly.

The obscured face of an older man sits in a director's chair.
Imprinted on the back of the chair is the name *Elia Kazan*.

The man in the director's chair, his face now clearly seen,
is ELIA KAZAN male white 55. He studies the scene.

                    ELIA KAZAN
          Cut! That was great. OK, let's
          break for lunch.

The film crew, camera operator, boom operator, and two actors
make their way off of the stage.

Budd, standing a few yards away from the stage, is approached
by Elia.

                    ELIA KAZAN (CONT'D)
          Budd, how are you? Glad you could
          stop by.

Elia extends his hand and Budd shakes it.

                    BUDD
          Gadge, good to see you.

                    ELIA KAZAN
          So what's going on my friend? You
          finish that novel you're working
          on?

                    BUDD
          Not yet, I'm slowly getting there.
          -- I've started a writing class.
          I'm looking for sponsors.

                    ELIA KAZAN
          OK, sounds good. Where's your
          class at?

                    BUDD
          Watts.

                    ELIA KAZAN
          Wow. Sounds tough.

                    BUDD
          It is.

                    ELIA KAZAN
          In for the long haul, huh?

                    BUDD
          Yeah, I am. -- Can I count on your
          support?

                    ELIA KAZAN
          Sure, Budd, you know that.
          Whatever you need.

                    BUDD
          Good.

Budd drapes his arm around Elia and they walk off stage
talking.

INT. WESTMINSTER NEIGHBORHOOD ASSOCIATION - ROOM - DAY

A group of Negroes are sitting in front of Budd. Among them
are Johnie Scott, Charles Johnson, and Eric Priestley.

                    BUDD
          Stories aren't fancy things.
          They're the things you've been
          doing, what you did in the uprising
          last month, what you're thinking
          about now.

                    ERIC
          About being homeless and living in
          a pool hall on Central Avenue.

                    BUDD
          I can't pretend to know what that's
          like.

                    ERIC
          All I heard was glass breaking. I
          went outside, there was ah angry
          crowd. It sounded like a swarm of
          bees. Vizzz, vizzz, vizzz, vizzz.

                    BUDD
          I had gone to Watts in my youth to
          hear T-Bone Walker and other local
          jazzmen in the honky tonks.
          Anybody heard of him?

                    JOHNIE
That's when Watts had class.
Central Avenue, back in the
forties. Yeah, the "Black belt of
the city." My mother told me about
it. Charlie Parker and Dizzie
Gillespie -- Now look at Watts.

                    BUDD
If I were to understand this urban
tragedy, it would require not
merely a look, but a lot of looks,
and not merely superficial looks
but finally, somehow, from the
inside looking out.

                    CHARLES
We've been turned inside out
alright.

                    BUDD
I'm impelled to produce
representations of Watts. You are
the representations of Watts.

                    JOHNIE
A Harvard dropout. I thought I was
getting away from the ghetto. I
was the first black from Watts to
go to Harvard.

                    BUDD
I'm here to organize and polish the
untrained language in which you
will turn the materials and events
of ghetto life into literature.

                    ERIC
You sure have a lot of confidence
in us.

                    BUDD
Extract the confidence with in
yourself. If you didn't have
confidence, you wouldn't be here.

Budd holds up several books for the class.

                    BUDD (CONT'D)
You are going to read these books
as part of your preparation.
                    (MORE)

                    BUDD (CONT'D)
          "Dark ghetto: dilemmas of social
          power." "Stranger in the Village,"
          "Narrative of the Life of Frederick
          Douglass," and "Autobiography of
          Malcolm X."

-- Budd holds up one other book.

                    BUDD (CONT'D)
          This is a mandatory read. Your
          first assignment. "Manchild in the
          Promised Land." A comprehensive
          survey of ghetto narrative and
          language. The development of
          Claude Brown as an urban
          intellectual. A template for the
          writing of a new cohort of urban
          intellectuals emerging from the
          damaged terrain of Watts.

                    CHARLES
          Sounds like a tough read. Good
          choice.

                    BUDD
          Though this is a writing class.
          From now on we will refer to this
          class as the "Watts Writers
          Workshop."

INT. WESTMINSTER NEIGHBORHOOD ASSOCIATION - OFFICE - DAY

Archie sits behind his desk shuffling through forms and
filling out paperwork when Budd walks in.

                    BUDD
          Hey, Archie. I thought I'd try, as
          a calling card, the film "On the
          Waterfront," that I had written.
          Since the street kids who are my
          prospective students have no money
          to go to the movies.

Archie with his head down, focused on the form he's filling
out, has yet to glance up.

                    BUDD (CONT'D)
          Maybe I could talk to the manager
          of a local theater, get'em to run
          the picture for us, at some off-
          theatrical hour that wouldn't
          compete with commercial showings.

Archie stops filling out paperwork and slowly lifts his head up.

>   ARCHIE
>   Don't you know there's no such
>   thing as a movie theater in Watts?
>   You've got to go all the way up to
>   midtown, a good ten or twelve
>   miles, about two dollars round trip
>   by bus.

>   BUDD
>   Um, I think I have an idea.

EXT. HOME OF JOHNIE SCOTT - PORCH - EVENING

Samuel stands next to Johnie who's holding a liquor bottle in one hand, and a red pill capsule in the palm of his other hand.

>   SAMUEL
>   What you gonna do with that red
>   devil?

>   JOHNIE
>   What do you think?

Johnie pops the red pill into his mouth and chases it with a swig of liquor.

>   SAMUEL
>   So what'd you think of Schulberg?

>   JOHNIE
>   He's cool. You should come and
>   check it out. Judge for yourself.

>   SAMUEL
>   Argh.

Johnie takes another swig of liquor, he holds out the liquor bottle to Samuel.

>   SAMUEL (CONT'D)
>   Nah, I'm cool. -- The niggas in
>   Watts are caught between the
>   cultural nationalists and the
>   revolutionary nationalists.
>   There's a tug-of-war going on.

Johnie sways slightly, speech slurred a little from the stupor he's in.

                    JOHNIE
          You should express that in writing.
          Share it at the workshop.

                    SAMUEL
          Workshop?

                    JOHNIE
          Yeah. The "Watts Writers
          Workshop," that's what it's called
          now.

Johnie reaches into his back pocket and pulls out a paper, he
unfolds it.

                    JOHNIE (CONT'D)
               (reading)
          Because it was never there,
          something empty filled the gap.
          And since the absence was not seen.
          All too soon the people died. They
          died as babies die...

Johnie quickly folds the paper up and stuffs it in his
pocket.

                    SAMUEL
          You wrote that?

                    JOHNIE
          Yeah.

                    SAMUEL
          Go on, finish. I wanna hear some
          more.

                    JOHNIE
          Nah.

Johnie takes another swig from the liquor bottle.

                    JOHNIE (CONT'D)
          I'm ah share it with the group.

                    SAMUEL
          Them red devils help you write?

                    JOHNIE
          It's a downer. Puts you in a
          hypnotic state. I wrote some cool
          shit while I was high.

                    SAMUEL
          Maybe I'll try it sometime.

EXT. WESTMINSTER NEIGHBORHOOD ASSOCIATION - EVENING

A lively group of Negro teens are carousing out front.

INT. WESTMINSTER NEIGHBORHOOD ASSOCIATION - ROOM - EVENING

Several Negro kids that are wearing boxing gloves engage in light sparring.

JIMMIE SHERMAN African American male 24 watches over them closely.

                    JIMMIE
          No, no. Don't drop your gloves,
          you'll leave yourself open.

Jimmie gets into an orthodox boxing stance.

                    JIMMIE (CONT'D)
          OK, everybody pay attention. Keep
          your guards up in a defensive
          posture, and jab...

Jimmie quickly flicks jabs with his left arm.

                    JIMMIE (CONT'D)
               (pausing)
          Just like that. Now try it.

The Negro kids paired in two's, jab at each other.

                    JIMMIE (CONT'D)
          That's it. Keep your guard up.

Budd walks in holding a paper in his hand.

                    BUDD
               (slight stammer)
          Jimmie Sherman. You want to train
          boxers or become a writer?

Jimmie stops what he's doing and looks at Budd.

                    JIMMIE
          Why can't I do both?

                    BUDD
          You can.

                    BUDD (CONT'D)
          I have your application for the
          workshop here. There's something
          on here that really struck me.

Budd reads from the paper in his hand.

                    BUDD (CONT'D)
          "I had made up verses since I was a
          little boy, but it was taking part
          in the Revolt of Watts and thinking
          about what it had meant to me for
          days afterward, that made me
          realize that what I really wanted
          to be was a writer, not just for
          myself but for all of us who want
          justice in America." -- Profound.

                    JIMMIE
          Does that mean I've been accepted?

EXT. WESTMINSTER NEIGHBORHOOD ASSOCIATION - EVENING

Archie walks out and confronts a lively group of Negro teens.

                    ARCHIE
          Hey, put out them cigarettes, toss
          the joints, and get rid of the
          beer. You guys come upstairs, Budd
          has something he wants you to check
          out.

INT. WESTMINSTER NEIGHBORHOOD ASSOCIATION - ASSEMBLY HALL

Budd is placing a reel of film onto a 16mm film projector.

The rowdy group of Negro teens meander their way in.

                    BUDD
          OK, everyone take a seat.

NEGRO TEEN #1 blares out...

                    NEGRO TEEN #1
          Aye, y'all, it's movie time.
          Where's the popcorn?

NEGRO TEEN #2 barks out...

                    NEGRO TEEN #2
          Budd, what we watching?

                    BUDD
          This film is called, "On the
          Waterfront."

                         NEGRO TEEN #2
               Aw, man, it sounds boring.

                         BUDD
               I won an Oscar for writing the
               screenplay.

                         NEGRO TEEN #1
               Bullshit, you, Oscar? Aye, y'all
               we gotta check this out.

That gets some laughs from the group of Negro teens.

                         BUDD
               There are life lessons in this film
               that you can apply to your own
               lives. Most of all, I want the
               film to inspire everyone here to
               write. -- Would someone turn off
               the light?

A Negro teen hits the light switch and Budd starts the film
projector.

Dust filters through the refraction of light that beams from
the film projector.

The group of Negro teens settle down as the titles of the
film *On the Waterfront* appear on the projection screen.

Suddenly a frantic NEGRO STAFF WORKER rushes in.

                         NEGRO STAFF WORKER
               Aye, there's ah angry crowd
               outside. There really pissed off.
               Something's going on.

The Negro Staff Worker races off.

The group of Negro teens jump out of their seats and rush
out.

Budd looking confused collects himself and hustles off.

EXT. WESTMINSTER NEIGHBORHOOD ASSOCIATION - STREET - NIGHT

In the middle of a stunned and bewildered crowd of Negroes is
a young NEGRO MOTHER, on her knees, she mourns the lifeless
body of her infant.

                         NEGRO MOTHER
               My, baby's dead. My baby's dead.

The Negro Mother lets out a horrific *scream*.

Negro Teen #1, Negro Teen #2, and Budd break through the crowd, there speechless at the site of what they see.

The Negro Mother wails as she rocks the lifeless body of the infant.

An ambulance pulls up and two white paramedics enter the fray. They try to resuscitate the infant, but it's no use.

Watching in the midst of the angry crowd the Negro Staff Worker expresses her frustration.

> NEGRO STAFF WORKER
> This place is in a worse depression
> than the country was in, back in
> the early thirties.

The Negro Staff Worker points to a two-story building that's cater-cornered, it's a mortuary.

> NEGRO STAFF WORKER (CONT'D)
> But that shop over there does the
> best business in town.

One of the paramedics drapes a white sheet over the dead infant.

The Negro Mother can only watch as her grief intensifies.

> NEGRO MOTHER
> Got damn it if you got here
> earlier. My baby would be alive.
> Cuz we live in Watts you don't give
> a fuck. General Hospital is a
> dozen fucken miles away...

Budd, his face flush, stares on as the angry tongue-lashing from the Negro Mother fades to a muffle.

INT. WESTMINSTER NEIGHBORHOOD ASSOCIATION - ASSEMBLY HALL

In the dark, the film projector is still running.

On the projection screen, the film *On the Waterfront* plays. The image of MARLON BRANDO stands out prominently on the screen as he intensely performs the lines...

> MARLON BRANDO
> *You don't understand. I coulda had*
> *class. I coulda been a contender.*
> (MORE)

                    MARLON BRANDO (CONT'D)
          I coulda been somebody, instead of
          a bum, which is what I am, let's
          face it.

INT. HOME OF BUDD SCHULBERG - EVENING

A social gathering of high-brows is taking place. The men
are dressed in Black tie. The women's attire is a little
more flexible than for men. Knee-to-floor-length gowns,
evening dresses, palazzo-cut pants, heels, flat dress shoes,
a clutch, and jewelry.

Budd stands with JAMES BALDWIN African American male 41, and
Elia Kazan.

                    BUDD
          Jimmy, the despair is contrasted by
          the glimmer of hope, you see.   I
          was drawn to help in the only way I
          knew how, through writing.

James, holding a drink in one hand and a cigarette in the
other.

                    JAMES BALDWIN
          These young people have never
          believed in the American image of
          the Negro and have never bargained
          with the Republic, and now they
          never will. There is no longer any
          basis on which to bargain.

Budd and Elia are listening intently to James.

                    ELIA KAZAN
          That's a rather bleak outlook,
          don't you think?

                    JAMES BALDWIN
          I must honestly confess that I go
          through those moments of
          disappointment when I have to
          recognize the fact, that there
          aren't enough white persons in our
          country who are willing to cherish
          democratic principles over
          privilege. But I'm grateful to God
          that some are left.

James raises his glass up to Budd.

                    BUDD
               (to Elia)
          Jimmy hovers between the non-
          violence stance of Martin Luther
          King and the "by any means
          necessary" stance of Malcolm X.

                    ELIA KAZAN
          Well, we're all here for the same
          cause. It's not just a good cause,
          but a great one.

Just then Geraldine walks up.

                    GERALDINE
          Jimmy, Gadge, how are you two?

                    ELIA KAZAN
          I'm fine Geraldine. But please,
          call me Elia.

                    GERALDINE
          Only Budd can call you Gadge, huh?

                    JAMES BALDWIN
          You look lovely, Geraldine.

                    GERALDINE
          I'm glad you could make it.

                    JAMES BALDWIN
          Of course. Whatever I can do to
          support Budd.

Geraldine takes Budd by the arm.

                    GERALDINE
          Can I steal him away for a minute?

                    JAMES BALDWIN
          What do you think Elia?

                    ELIA KAZAN
          Ah, I guess. He's all yours.

With drinks in their hands, standing together chatting are
RICHARD BURTON a white male 40, and STEVE ALLEN a white male
44.

Geraldine walks up her arm wrapped around Budd's arm.

                    GERALDINE
          Richard, Steve, how are you two
          getting along?

                    RICHARD BURTON
We're fine.

                    GERALDINE
Look who I have with me.

                    BUDD
The hostess has me making my
rounds.

                    STEVE ALLEN
Geraldine you have organized a
great party. Budd, where would you
be without her?

                    BUDD
I have no idea.

                    STEVE ALLEN
I was just telling Richard, I want
to book both of you to come on the
show.

                    BUDD
Anytime, that would be great.

                    STEVE ALLEN
Richard can talk about his new
movie. You can bring us up to
speed on what you're working on.

                    RICHARD BURTON
Speaking of that. How are things
with this, ah, workshop you
started?

                    BUDD
It started off slow. I'm gaining
their trust. A white man in Watts
isn't a welcome site.

                    GERALDINE
         (light-hearted)
Steve, I'm a little insulted.

                    STEVE ALLEN
Oh.

                    GERALDINE
I have an upcoming movie myself. I
need the publicity.

                    STEVE ALLEN
I'll make a note of that.

                    RICHARD BURTON
          So, Budd. How do you find time for
          other projects with the workshop
          consuming all of your time?

                    BUDD
          I manage. I'm working on a novel
          in my spare time.

                    STEVE ALLEN
          What are your, ah, operating
          expenses for the workshop?

                    BUDD
          I'm funding it myself. So the out-
          of-pocket expenses vary.

                    RICHARD BURTON
          All that changes tonight. Look
          around, all your Hollywood friends
          are here to contribute.

A man sits at a piano playing *Ain't Misbehavin' as* guests
puff on cigarettes and sip drinks while listening.

INT. WESTMINSTER NEIGHBORHOOD ASSOCIATION - ROOM - DAY

Packed to capacity, an overflow crowd of Negroes spill into
the hallway.

Most of the Negroes are seated, while the others lean against
the wall.

Johnie Scott stands in the midst of seated Negroes, his eyes
fixed on a paper he's holding.

                    JOHNIE
          ...The unmarked graves are empty,
          as empty as the town that lies
          buried within them. We cry for
          opportunity, for freedom now! We
          scream for respect, human rights,
          and yet once gained we still hold a
          rebellious enmity: There is no
          feeling in this world, there was
          not ever...
               (looks up)
          ...never noticed.

As Johnie sits down in his chair, FANNIE CAROLE BROWN African
American female 22 stands up. Holding notebook papers in her
hand...

                    FANNIE
          I'm Fannie Brown, and this is my
          poem. "The Realization of a Dream
          Deferred." It happened; a success.
          Why then do I remain emotionless?
          From beneath many a strata-strata
          of bewilderment. Strata of
          disillusionment. Strata of lost
          hope. Self-pity. Self-doubt. It
          burst forth. And now. It
          happened; a success. But why do I
          yet remain emotionless?

Like the game Whac-A-Mole, Fannie sits down in a chair and
HARLEY MIMS a 40-year-old fair skin African American quickly
stands up from a chair. He opens a notebook.

                    HARLEY
          I'm Harley Mims, and this is an
          excerpt from my novel-in-progress,
          "Memoirs of a Shoeshine Boy."
          "Come on, nigger buddy," my pal
          Charly said to me; "we're going
          down to one of these fine hotels
          and pass for white." I damned near
          pissed on myself right there.
          "Just how in the hell are two ebony-
          hued, liver-lipped bastards like us
          gonna do it-tell ourselves ghost
          stories until we turn pale with
          fright and then run up to one of
          these white cafes? And suppose our
          real color comes back to us while
          we're drinking coffee? What
          happens then?" "Nothing like that,
          old nigger buddy." "Will you
          please stop calling me your nigger
          buddy? We're colored folks!"

Budd, holding onto some notes, stands in front of the
Negroes. They have a look of anticipation as if waiting to
hear something special.

                    BUDD
               (slight stammer)
          Thank you, Johnie, Fannie, and
          Harley.

Budd takes some glasses from the breast pocket of his short
sleeve shirt and puts them on. -- Looking at his notes.

                    BUDD (CONT'D)
          It takes courage to share. Words
          have an intimate connection to the
          person that's listening, even more
          so, to the person that's speaking.
          It's very personal. If you do
          nothing more than write clearly,
          you're going to be in the top ten
          percent of all writers. Don't try
          to sound impressive, just try to be
          clear. Don't obsess over your
          writing style, just try to be
          clear. Don't try to be anything
          other than clear, and you'll be
          good.

EXT. WATTS HAPPENING COFFEE HOUSE - DAY

A crude hand-painted sign stands out, as a mash-up of
concerned voices, Elaine Brown, Stanley Crouch, and James
Woods emanate from inside.

                    ELAINE BROWN (V.O.)
          Matt Diamond donated this building
          to the community, for us.

                    STANLEY CROUCH (V.O.)
          I harbor some resentment too. But
          what are you gonna tell the dude,
          he ain't welcome here?

                    JAMES (V.O.)
          I don't know what this guy's aim
          is...

INT. WATTS HAPPENING COFFEE HOUSE - CONTINUOUS

Looking a bit flustered is ELAINE BROWN, a fair skin
attractive African American female 22. With an astute look
and wearing glasses is STANLEY CROUCH an African American
male 20.

James Woods overly dramatic is agitated.

                    JAMES
          ...He's still an outsider. In no
          time this dude has gone from being
          under suspicion to being embraced
          by some of Watts most talented
          writers.

Standing just out of sight, Jayne Cortez steps forward, she
has a quizzical look on her face.

> JAYNE
> He's pushing cultural production
> through cultural liberalism. The
> Office of Economic Opportunity
> doesn't see that as a solution to
> employment, education, and juvenile
> delinquency.

> STANLEY CROUCH
> Dollars are being pumped into
> Watts. Cultural programs are a
> target for social reform. That's
> what liberal politicians are
> pushing for.

> ELAINE BROWN
> It's an experiment. They don't
> want to see another riot. You
> can't separate the black arts
> movement from black power
> activists. The eyes of the world
> are on Watts right now.

INT. L.A. FEDERAL BUREAU OF INVESTIGATION - OFFICE - DAY

A *dossier* is tossed onto a desk with the name *Budd Schulberg*
on it.

FBI Special Agent WILL HEATON male white 26 picks it up, he
thumbs through it. Inside are photos of Budd Schulberg with
Johnie Scott, Charles Johnson, and Eric Priestley standing in
front of the Westminster Neighborhood Association building.

Standing in front of Will Heaton is FBI Special Agent MICHAEL
QUINN male white 25.

> MICHAEL QUINN
> Schulberg was a "friendly witness"
> before the House Un-American
> Activities Committee, "naming
> names" in the early nineteen
> fifties.

> WILL HEATON
> (sarcastic)
> And now he's working with the
> brothers in Watts.

                    MICHAEL QUINN
The Black cultural programs are a
breeding ground for black
activists.

                    WILL HEATON
And that's a problem. The question
is, is Schulberg helping them plan
subversive activities?

                    MICHAEL QUINN
Ah, I don't think so, not
wittingly.

                    WILL HEATON
The Negroes have their own
language. They incorporate it into
music, dance, art. It's right in
Schulberg's face, he may be unaware
of the hidden messages.

                    MICHAEL QUINN
Like jungle drums?

                    WILL HEATON
That's a crude way of putting it,
but yeah. We have to get inside,
we need a black to do that, and not
just any black. For now, keep
surveilling all the cultural
programs in Watts and report back
to me. Good job.

INT. WATTS HAPPENING COFFEE HOUSE - DAY

As if in church, a Negro man's finger strides over piano
keys. Stanley Crouch is on the drums, and Jayne Cortez bangs
a tambourine in rhythm against the palm of her hand.

Elaine Brown with a microphone in her hand belts out a
spiritual hymn.

                    ELAINE BROWN
          (singing)
     Yes, I remember, the yesterdays.
     The poverty that you and me
     survived. For we tried living on
     streets that weren't giving. I'd
     laugh and cried, in youth, we died
     and didn't know. Oh yes, my
     friends, our history, the memory
     shall carry me until we're free.
                    (MORE)

> ELAINE BROWN (CONT'D)
> *The times we saw, we didn't*
> *deserve. Hostility, we couldn't*
> *see, it was absurd. But we gave*
> *joy, each girl and boy, so innocent*
> *our future bent against the wind.*
> *Oh yes, my friends, our history,*
> *the memory shall carry me until*
> *we're free...*

Several yards away watching are Budd, Charles, Eric, Jimmie, and Johnie.

Samuel walks up and greets Johnie with the black handshake.

> JOHNIE
> What's up brotha, finally decided
> to come.
> (turns to Budd)
> Budd, this is Samuel, your newest
> recruit.

Budd and Samuel shake hands with an act of familiarity.

> SAMUEL
> I thought y'all was at Westminster?

> BUDD
> We outgrew the place, so we're
> using the Coffee House for now.

> JOHNIE
> That's Charles, Eric, and Jimmie.

Samuel, Charles, Eric, and Jimmie acknowledge each other with head nods, and the black power fist pump.

Suddenly walking within a few feet of Budd are two word smiths, a NEGRO GUY, and NEGRO GIRL. They direct their rhythmic animosity at Budd.

> NEGRO GIRL
> Look at them flames lightin' up the
> sky, ain't neva seen flames
> shootin' up so high.

> NEGRO GUY
> Are you listenin' people to what
> I'm sayin'. Cuz it show looks to
> me like dem niggas ain't playin'.

> NEGRO GIRL
> Dem niggas ain't playing.

                    NEGRO GUY
Dem niggas ain't playing.

                    NEGRO GIRL
Dem niggas ain't playing.

                    NEGRO GUY
Ever since they passed them civil
rights. Those fires have been
lighting up the nights. And this
city ain't gonna stop till we all
have equal rights. Looks to me
like dem niggas ain't playin'.

                    NEGRO GIRL
Dem niggas ain't playing.

                    NEGRO GUY
Dem niggas ain't playin'.

                    NEGRO GIRL
Dem niggas ain't playin'.

                    NEGRO GUY
Looks like they developed ah new
black pride. It even show in the
way they now stride. You better
look around y'all can't you see
what I'm sayin'. Show looks to me
like dem niggas ain't playing.

                    NEGRO GIRL
Dem niggas ain't playing.

                    NEGRO GUY
Dem niggas ain't playin'.

                    NEGRO GIRL
Dem niggas ain't playin'.

                    NEGRO GUY
I think they tryna to get sumthin'
started.

                    NEGRO GIRL
Oh, yeah.

                    NEGRO GUY
I'm talkin' about SNCC and US, and
the Black Panther Party. Is anyone
listening to what I'm sayin'. Cuz
it show looks to me like dem niggas
ain't playin'.

The Negro Guy and the Negro Girl give Budd a smug look and give each other five as they walk away joining Elaine, Jayne, and Stanley.

                    SAMUEL
               (turns to Budd)
          That was the welcoming committee.
          They wanted to make you feel right
          at home.

EXT. NBC STUDIOS - DAY

A car pulls up to the guard shack. The guard gives some hand gestures and the car pulls off.

The car pulls into a parking stall. STUART SCHULBERG male white 43, and Budd Schulberg get out of the car.

As they walk...

                    STUART SCHULBERG
          He liked the pitch. Especially
          coming off the riots. This is
          something that will captivate the
          country...

INT. NBC STUDIOS - OFFICE - DAY

A nameplate sits atop a desk, inscribed on it is, *Don Durgin President of NBC Television*.

Sitting behind the desk is DON DURGIN male white 43. The phone on the desk *buzzes*, and Don picks up.

                    DON DURGIN
          Yeah, OK, send them in.

Stuart and Budd walk in. Don stands up to greet them.

                    DON DURGIN (CONT'D)
          Hey, Stuart. How are you?

                    STUART SCHULBERG
          Good, Good, this is my brother
          Budd.

Don and Budd shake hands.

                    DON DURGIN
          Nice to meet you, Budd. Sit down,
          sit down.

Stuart and Budd have a seat in front of Don.

                    DON DURGIN (CONT'D)
          I'll tell you, that movie On the
          Waterfront, that's one of my
          favorite movies. That line from
          Marlon Brando, "I coulda been a
          contender. I coulda been
          somebody." I understand Marlon
          improvised that line.

                    BUDD
          Yeah, that's true.

                    DON DURGIN
          Classic -- That's enough of my
          rambling. So, Stuart and I have
          been talking about a documentary.
          I really like the idea, what would
          be your approach is what I want to
          know.

                    BUDD
          It would be pretty straightforward.
          There's something about the burning
          of Los Angeles that had been in the
          air for a long time. It broke on
          the news program, from that moment
          on everybody in Los Angeles was
          glued to their TV sets...

                    DON DURGIN
          ...You started a writer's workshop
          in Watts.

                    BUDD
          That's right. The interest in
          writing was amazing, just amazing.
          It was like all of Watts can write.
          Actually, an awful lot of people
          had a lot to say, some of them can
          say it most effectively.

                    DON DURGIN
          Um, we need to play the angles. "A
          Hollywood writer reaches back to
          lift up the voices of Watts." --
          Stuart, run with it. Budd whatever
          you need just let me know.

INT. WATTS HAPPENING COFFEE HOUSE - DAY

Elaine Brown walks up with a magazine in her hand.

                    ELAINE BROWN
                  (reading)
          Every Friday afternoon, Novelist
          and Screenwriter Budd Schulberg
          leaves his tree-shaded home in
          North Beverly Hills and drives
          across town to the Negro slum of
          Watts. There, at the Watts
          Happening Coffee House, a
          ramshackle building across the
          street from the charred foundation
          of a store razed in last year's
          riots, the author of "What Makes
          Sammy Run?" sits down for three
          hours with a small group of ghetto-
          scarred Negroes and teaches them
          how to write poetry, plays, short
          stories, and novels. A one-time
          teacher of creative writing at
          Columbia, Schulberg says that their
          writing ability is "so much higher
          than my group of college students."

Standing together are Johnie, Jimmie, and Samuel.

                    JOHNIE
          Read that last part again.

Elaine frowns, Johnie walks up to her.

                    JOHNIE (CONT'D)
          Can I see that?

Elaine, frowning, her lips pursed, hands the magazine to
Johnie, he looks over the cover.

                    JOHNIE (CONT'D)
          Huh, Time Magazine.

Johnie looks at the inside page of the magazine.

                    JOHNIE (CONT'D)
                  (reading)
          Schulberg says that their writing
          ability is "so much higher than my
          group of college students."

                    ELAINE BROWN
          That white man really got y'all
          fooled.

                    JOHNIE
          Ay, Leumas...
                  (turns to Elaine)
                  (MORE)

                    JOHNIE (CONT'D)
He changed his name, it's Leumas
now.
         (reading)
Schulberg is equally high on the
talents of Leumas Sirrah eighteen,
a high-school student whose poems
are generally lyrical abstractions
about God and life, and Jimmy
Sherman, twenty-two, whose four-
stanza verse TH' WORKIN' MACHINE is
being set to music by television's
Steve Allen.

                    ELAINE BROWN
That article demeans y'all while it
praises him as some sort of savior.

Johnie turns to Jimmie.

                    JOHNIE
         (flippant)
Jimmie, how much is Steve Allen
paying you?

SONORA MCKELLER, a sassy African American in her 50s walks in
holding a half pint of liquor.

                    JOHNIE (CONT'D)
Ay, Sonora you read the article
yet?
         (holds up magazine)
They have a quote in here from you.
         (reading)
"At first people were skeptical as
to why he was down here," says
Sonora McKeller, one of Schulberg's
regulars. "But it's different when
you find that a person is dedicated
and might well be somewhere else
making money."

As if she didn't hear Johnie. Sonora sips from the liquor
bottle.

                    SONORA MCKELLER
I'm I early? Where's Budd?

                    SAMUEL
Elaine, why don't you join our
group?

                         JIMMIE
          Yeah, you should. You all uptight
          about a white man who's opening
          doors for us.

Just then Budd walks in.

                         ELAINE BROWN
                    (clapping)
          There he is, the great white hope.

INT. WATTS HAPPENING COFFEE HOUSE - CONTINUOUS

As if two opposing teams are sharing one large space. Elaine
and her group of Negro artists are on one side and Budd and
his group of Negro writers are on the other side.

Budd sits at the head of the semi-circle surrounded by Jimmie
Sherman, Samuel Harris "now Leumas Sirrah," Sonora McKeller,
Charles Johnson, Johnie Scott, Eric Priestley, and several
other Negroes.

                         BUDD
          There are some things I want to
          discuss, some of which you may not
          be receptive to. I've applied for
          a grant from the Rockefeller
          Foundation. I had to prepare a
          report for them. They have
          concerns about extreme militant
          points of view in your writings.

                         SAMUEL
          Awe, man Elaine was right.

                         BUDD
          Samuel...

                         SAMUEL
          ...It's Leumas dig, Leumas Sirrah.
          That's what I go by now.

Budd looks taken aback. The glare from Negroes in the
writer's group pierces through Budd, he feels their anger.

                         BUDD
          It's not my intent to constrict
          your writing style. But Black
          Nationalism is perceived as a
          threat by many philanthropic
          organizations.

                         ERIC
          Who gives a shit? You come up here
          wanting to liberate our voice. Now
          you want to muzzle us.

                         BUDD
          These organizations that support
          anti-poverty programs are worried
          that grants are being used either
          to underwrite militant activity or
          simply disappearing into the
          pockets of corrupt poverty program
          administrators.

Jimmie in a mocking slave voice.

                         JIMMIE
          You wouldn't be talkin' bout us
          would yah sir? Cuz we don't want
          to cause' no trouble sir.

                         CHARLES
          They don't have to worry about me.
          I'm a pacifist -- By nature that
          is.

                         JOHNIE
          It doesn't make a difference.
          We'll never get from under the
          microscope of the man.

                         BUDD
          I had to bring this up. I'm not
          looking at a bunch of radicals. If
          we want to expand and grow, Black
          Nationalism must remain on the page
          as it relates to our writer's
          group.

Sonora stands up from her chair and holds up her liquor
bottle.

                    SONORA MCKELLER
               (tipsy)
          You see this here bottle. Theirs a
          lot of troubles in here. And it
          all comes out on the got damn page,
          you hear me.

                         BUDD
          Yes, Sonora, I hear you.

                    SONORA MCKELLER
          OK.

Sonora takes a sip from the liquor bottle and sits down.

                    BUDD
          Discussion is good. It's an
          excising process. I have some good
          news that I hope you'll all
          embrace. NBC television is going
          to fund a documentary on the Watts
          Writers Workshop, how about that?

The group of Negro writers erupt enthusiastically.

From across the large space. The joyous commotion interrupts
Elaine and her Negro group of artists. They stop in the
midst of acting, dancing, painting, and playing musical
instruments.

Elaine's eyebrows furrow and a curious look of resentment is
etched on her face.

EXT. WATTS - WILL ROGERS PARK - DAY

Looking ultra cool, and vibrating to the sounds of Jazz
Music. A sizeable crowd of Negroes of all ages sport afros,
and African braided hairstyles, and some are wearing colorful
dashiki shirts.

Other male Negroes are wearing the everyday attire of slim-
fit trousers, button-down shirts, loafers, Fedora hats, and
dark shades.

As well, some of the Negro women are wearing everyday fits
such as cigarette pants, pencil skirts, and open and closed-
toe flats.

On a makeshift stage with iron railings, a band is
performing. On the piano grimacing as he strikes the keys is
HORACE TAPSCOTT, an African American male 32, he reminds you
of a young Samuel L Jackson in appearance.

The Jazz band looks slick and hip as they perform on a
rendering of *The Giant Is Awakened,* the saxophonist blows,
and Stanley Crouch strums on the drums.

As the band concludes their set the crowd gives them a warm
round of applause. Horace steps from behind the piano and
walks up to the microphone.

                    HORACE TAPSCOTT
          Thank you very much. Some of you
          know me from my music.
                    (MORE)

                    HORACE TAPSCOTT (CONT'D)
          For those that don't, I'm Horace
          Tapscott, and behind me is my band
          the "Pan Afrikan Peoples
          Arkestra"...

Separated about twenty yards from each other. Disguised like
hippies, FBI Special Agents Michael Quinn and BRANDON CLEARY
male white 26 move through the crowd. Some Negroes pick up
on their conspicuous presents and some don't.

                    HORACE TAPSCOTT (O.C.) (CONT'D)
          ...I'm not just a musician, but a
          community activist, teacher, and
          mentor. I've formed the
          Underground Musicians Association
          (UGMA).

Brandon Cleary subtly adjusts his hat which conceals a micro
audio transmitter.

                    BRANDON CLEARY
          Quinn, are you getting this?

Michael Quinn has now situated himself near the stage. He
adjusts his dark shades which are actually an audio recorder
and camera.

                    MICHAEL QUINN
          He's coming in loud and clear.

                    HORACE TAPSCOTT
          ...I cater specifically to the
          community, playing in juvenile
          centers, prisons, churches,
          hospitals, and children's homes.
          "It's all about artists of like
          minds involved in developing their
          art form and, at the same time,
          having social consciousness and a
          sense of responsibility." Were
          going to take a fifteen-minute
          break. Then will be back to
          perform another set for you.

Horace walks off stage, and there to greet him is Elaine
Brown.

                    ELAINE BROWN
          Hey, Horace man, that was a groovy
          set.

Horace and Elaine give each other the black power handshake.

                    HORACE TAPSCOTT
          Thank, you, sista. We gonna have
          to cut a record together.

                    ELAINE BROWN
          I'm ready, you know I am.

Just then Stanley Crouch walks up.

                    STANLEY CROUCH
          Elaine, what's happening?

                    ELAINE BROWN
          Stanley, you was doing your thang
          on those drums.

                    STANLEY CROUCH
          What do you think about the turnout
          today?

                    ELAINE BROWN
          It's beautiful man. Seeing our
          people together like this is what
          it's all about.

A few yards away observing Horace, Elaine, and Stanley is
Michael Quinn.

                    MICHAEL QUINN
               (fiddling with shades)
          Brandon, I can't pick up what
          they're saying.

                    BRANDON CLEARY (V.O.)
          Well, move in closer.

                    MICHAEL QUINN
          If I do that. I'll blow my cover.

                    BRANDON CLEARY (V.O.)
          Make sure you get photos of them.

                    MICHAEL QUINN
          Oh, I've got'em covered from every
          angle.

Horace, Elaine, and Stanley are actively engaged.

                    ELAINE BROWN
          Ay, man, it's been a while since
          you've come down to the coffee
          house.

                    STANLEY CROUCH
          Yeah, man, we get new students all
          the time. They'd be thrilled to
          have you work with them.

                    HORACE TAPSCOTT
          Yeah, yeah, it'll be sooner than
          later...

Michael Quinn adjusts his glasses getting some clear photos
of Horace, Elaine, and Stanley.

INT. L.A. FEDERAL BUREAU OF INVESTIGATION - CONFERENCE ROOM

A hand tacks a clear black and white photo of Horace
Tapscott, Elaine Brown, and Stanley Crouch onto a planning
board.

The hand pulls back revealing FBI Special Agent Will Heaton.

                    WILL HEATON
          Any kind of black militancy or
          black consciousness or anything
          that disturbs the status quo has to
          be crushed.

Sitting in chairs facing Will are FBI Special Agents Michael
Quinn and Brandon Cleary, now looking clean cut wearing
suits. Several other clean-cut Agents sit at attention, all
eyes fixed on Will.

                    WILL HEATON (CONT'D)
               (using pointer)
          Elaine Brown is a member of the
          Black Panther Party, she also has
          ties to the Cultural Nationalist US
          Organization.

An assortment of other photos are arrayed all over the
planning board. Negroes loitering in front of Studio Watts,
the Watts Happening Coffee House, and the Westminster
Neighborhood Association.

                    WILL HEATON (CONT'D)
               (using pointer)
          There is a cross-affiliation among
          these subversives, an
          interconnection.

Closeup photos of Budd Schulberg with Johnie Scott. Other
close-up photos of Jayne Cortez with James Woods and Horace
Tapscott.

                    WILL HEATON (CONT'D)
          These organizations all operate in
          a concentrated dense area.
          Specifically one-hundred and third
          street.

                    MICHAEL QUINN
          The US Organization is directly
          involved with the Mafundi Institute
          and is connected to the coffee
          house.

                    BRANDON CLEARY
          I suggest we try to pit them
          against each other.
                    (looking at notes)
          The Black Panther Party and the US
          Organization have differing
          ideological views. The BPP
          endorses radicalism, and US pushes
          culturalism. The workshops are in
          essence "fronts" to advance their
          agendas.

                    WILL HEATON
          Let's focus on fracturing any
          alliance between them, causing the
          groups to turn on each other.

                    MICHAEL QUINN
          Government agencies are pouring
          dollars and political backing into
          these programs. Schulberg is a
          well-known Hollywood screenwriter
          with a wealth of media and
          political connections.

                    WILL HEATON
          Who gives a damn?. I want to
          employ every tactic to accomplish
          the FBI's mission. Everyone here
          needs to understand that.

INT. WATTS HAPPENING COFFEE HOUSE - DAY

Voices merge with the rhythm of congas and calypso drums.
The resonant sounds all seem to sync together.

Stuart directs a camera operator and boom operator over to a
large sofa.

Budd sits in the middle surrounded on either side by Charles, Eric, Jimmie, Johnie, Sonora, Samuel and HARRY DOLAN, a portly 29-year-old African American.

> HARRY DOLAN
> I was attending Los Angeles Harbor College when the Watts riots erupted...

> SAMUEL
> Uprising, brotha, uprising.

> HARRY DOLAN
> ...I hear you, brotha, I hear you. -- A reference to Budd Schulberg's Watts Writers Workshop in Jet magazine prompted me to join the workshop. So now I'm here.

> BUDD
> Freedom to write can be a complex concept. In some cases, it may be considered absolute freedom.

Harry opens a notebook he is holding.

> HARRY DOLAN
> I want to share a passage from "Will There Be Another Riot in Watts?"

> SAMUEL
> Uprising, man...

> HARRY DOLAN
> ...I hear you, Leumas.
>   (reading)
> -- No, not as the riot of last summer, not as a spontaneous, frustrated explosive reaction in death indiscriminately. No, this will not happen again, for "the niggers and criminal elements" that fought and died learned their lessons well...

MONTAGE.

-- Stuart now directs the camera operator and boom operator to cover the painters as they stand at easels creating wonderful works of art...

-- Negro men and women are engaged in modern dance as the camera operator and boom operator cover James Woods giving instructions.

-- Negro men and women looking extremely hip sitting in rows of arranged folding chairs watch as Negro musicians wearing crew neck short sleeve knitted shirts play percussion instruments on a small stage.

-- Stuart directs the camera operator and boom operator to move in close capturing the intense playing of the congas and calypso drums.

END MONTAGE.

EXT. HOME OF BUDD SCHULBERG - PORCH - DAY

A postal carrier bag slung over their shoulder walks up. The postal carrier pulls envelopes from the bag and thumbs through them when the front door opens. Geraldine steps out...

                    GERALDINE
          Oh, I'll take those.

The postal carrier hands the envelopes to Geraldine.

                    GERALDINE (CONT'D)
          Thank you.

Geraldine quickly looks over the envelopes walks back inside and shuts the door.

INT. HOME OF BUDD SCHULBERG - OFFICE

With glasses on his face and a focused expression, Budd sits at his desk pecking away at the typewriter when Geraldine walks in.

                    GERALDINE
          How's it going?

Budd pauses and pulls the glasses down from his face.

                    BUDD
          OK. Trying to finish up so I can
          send the manuscript over to the
          publisher.

                    GERALDINE
          I have something here that may
          interest you.

Geraldine hands Budd a stack of envelopes, he carefully scans them over stopping on one particular envelope that reads, *National Foundation for the Arts.*

Putting back on his glasses. Budd opens the envelope and pulls out the letter.

                    BUDD
               (reading aloud)
          Mr. Schulberg, we are pleased to
          inform you that your grant request
          for twenty-five thousand has been
          approved. These funds will match
          the award grant from the
          Rockefeller Foundation...

Budd pulls down his glasses and stands up from his chair.

                    GERALDINE
          I had my doubts. You were spending
          your own money to fund the
          workshop. Calling in support from
          friends. It all seemed so
          burdensome.

                    BUDD
          And now?

                    GERALDINE
          You are a selfless wonderful
          person.

                    BUDD
          Is that why you married me?

                    GERALDINE
          That was part of it.

Budd and Geraldine hug giving each other a light kiss on the lips.

EXT. WATTS - 9807 BEACH STREET - DAY

Budd, Johnie, and Harry Dolan are standing out front looking at the place with a sense of appreciation.

                    JOHNIE
          Wow, Budd, this is too cool. Our
          own spot.

                    BUDD
          What do you think Harry?

                    HARRY DOLAN
Being able to come here and work
with such a creative group, is
cool, real cool.

                    JOHNIE
Then you don't mind doubling as the
janitor?

                    HARRY DOLAN
C'mon, man, I was a janitor for
City Hall. This is a piece of
cake.

INT. WATTS - 9807 BEACH STREET - DAY

In a communal environment Charles, Eric, Jimmie, Sonora,
Samuel, Harley Mims, Fannie Carole Brown, ALVIN SAXON JR.,
African American 19, and a few other Negro writers all
interact examining each other's notebooks.

Budd walks in, followed by Johnie, and Harry Dolan.

                    SAMUEL
There he is. The man of the hour.

                    ERIC
Right on Budd. This place is hip.

                    JIMMIE
The coffee house is cool, but this
new place is righteous.

                    BUDD
Thank you, everyone, but this is a
collective effort. The grant made
it possible to purchase this house.

                    CHARLES
It's a beautiful thing man, a
beautiful thing.

                    BUDD
Most of you know each other...

                    ALVIN SAXON JR.
...Excuse me, Mr. Schulberg, I'm
new to the group. My government
name is Alvin Saxon Jr. but my
African name is Ojenke. It means
sacrifice, innovative, powerful.

                         BUDD
          OK, thank you for that -- Ojenke.
          Now, I'm assigning Johnie to work
          with poets in the small guesthouse
          in the back. Here in the front,
          I'll work with those interested in
          writing short stories, essays, and
          novels. I'm naming Harry Dolan as
          my director of the workshop. This
          is not just a meeting space for the
          writing programs but also will
          provide housing for some of the
          Workshop members.

Sonora walks up to Budd and hands him a fifth of unopened
brown liquor.

                    SONORA MCKELLER
          Budd, I know you don't drink, but
          please accept this.

                         BUDD
          Why, thank you Sonora. I'll save
          this for a special occasion.

                    SONORA MCKELLER
          What do you think this is?

                        FANNIE
               (looking at watch)
          Ay, it's almost time.

                        HARLEY
          Yeah, turn the tv on.

Everyone's attention turns to a 25-inch television set. Budd
turns it on.

The NBC Peacock logo appears, music fades in and the voice of
the BROADCASTER is heard.

                    BROADCASTER (V.O.)
          The following program is brought to
          you in living color, on NBC.

Credits begin to roll on top of a Pacific Union freight
train. THE ANGRY VOICES OF WATTS, With BUDD SCHULBERG
Produced and Directed by STUART SCHULBERG...

On the television screen, Budd is seen sitting on the sofa
with Charles, Eric, Jimmie, Johnie, Sonora, Samuel, and
Harry.

                         BUDD
          *All of us, who, who have gathered
          here. You're in the, in the coffee
          house. Ah, wondered, both about
          the long-range and the immediate,
          ah, prospects. Just because I've
          been involved in the workshop,
          everybody asks me, as is if I
          possibly could know. Will there be
          another revolt...*

*Samuel appears on the television screen looking cool, wearing
dark shades and a long sleeve button-down shirt. He's
leaning over a pool table, pool stick in hand he lines up a
shot.*

                        SAMUEL
          *So being a writer means being
          someone who has developed self-
          awareness about what they do and
          why they do it.*

*On the television screen, Jimmie sits on the sofa among Budd,
Charles, Eric, Johnie, Sonora, Samuel, and Harry, he has a
calm solemn look about himself.*

                        JIMMIE
                    (recites poem)
          *I cried, I smiled. I'm here, I'm
          glad I'm here, despite the bitter
          pain and fear. The pain feels
          good. Good, I'm here...*

Johnie, Harry, Charles, Eric, Jimmie, Sonora, Samuel, Harley
Mims, Fannie Carole Brown, Alvin Saxon Jr., and the other
Negro writers are all silently fixated on the television set.

INT. FEDERAL BUILDING - DAY

Harry, Budd, and Johnie sit before a panel of spectacle
donning suit-wearing white politicians led by Senator ABRAHAM
RIBICOFF male, 66.

                    ABRAHAM RIBICOFF
          There are a number of anti-poverty
          programs in place. With funds
          allocated specifically for Watts.
          For budgetary concerns, the
          oversight committee must review and
          determine the validity and
          sustainability of these programs.
                       (MORE)

                    ABRAHAM RIBICOFF (CONT'D)
          Can you share with us, from your
          perspective, since you and Mr.
          Dolan have directly benefited from
          these programs?

                    JOHNIE
          I want to address arts programs,
          primarily their ability to
          transform mental attitudes that
          have hampered Negro advancement.
          Creative writing has the power to
          transform Negroes relationship with
          American society by opening new
          linguistic vistas. Community
          members want precisely such
          intellectual stimulation. I had a
          conversation with a Negro social
          worker, I demanded that they do not
          send "any more baseball players or
          prize-fighters." That is not just
          my sentiment, but the sentiment of
          the community at large.

                    ABRAHAM RIBICOFF
          Thank you, Mr. Scott. Mr. Dolan,
          you witnessed the riots...

                    HARRY DOLAN
          ...Uprising, Mr. Ribicoff.

                    ABRAHAM RIBICOFF
             (clears throat)
          Yes -- You and Mr. Scott have
          recognized published works. It's
          obvious that cultural programs can
          work, you are a testament to that.
          What more can you add?

                    HARRY DOLAN
          Cultural efforts are a broader
          approach to urban reform. It's not
          the answer to issues like health
          care, housing, transportation,
          juvenile delinquency. Urban unrest
          is the main concern of American
          politics. The culture programs
          help quell that unrest.

                    ABRAHAM RIBICOFF
          Thank, you, Mr. Dolan. Mr.
          Schulberg, you spearheaded this
          workshop initially, unaided by
          government sponsorship.
                    (MORE)

> ABRAHAM RIBICOFF (CONT'D)
> Where do you see this cultural
> renaissance going?

> BUDD
> I argue for ending inequality,
> exacerbated by flawed urban
> planning, and for increasing
> national investment in the arts.
> It's not a means to an end but a
> conduit to opportunity.

INT. WATTS - 9807 BEACH STREET - DAY

Perturbed, Sonora stands in the midst of a large group of
Negro writers.

> SONORA MCKELLER
> The stream of money that flows into
> the workshop is being misused or
> ripped off.

Harry Dolan stands up from his chair, his brow is sweaty, he
pulls a handkerchief from the pocket of his blazer, wiping
his forehead.

> HARRY DOLAN
> Sonora, the tremendous amounts of
> cash you're jaw-jacking about
> really is a product of your
> imagination.

Harry twirls a fat cigar between his thumb and forefinger.

> HARRY DOLAN (CONT'D)
> I will account for every cent
> spent...

Budd sitting at the head of the group of Negro writers
interjects.

> BUDD
> (stammering)
> ...Harry, I think we can deal with
> business matters later. Now it's
> time for the writers.

Harry and Sonora both sit down, and no sooner than they do
the sound of footsteps is heard coming from the roof.

> HARRY DOLAN
> Oh, man, that boy.

A loud thud of something heavy hitting the ground is heard. The side window raises up, a leg comes through, then the whole torso, it's Samuel.

> SONORA MCKELLER
> Man, can't you come through the
> front door like everyone else?

> SAMUEL
> I'm superstitious.

> BUDD
> Leumas, please take a seat. -- OK,
> who has a poem that they would like
> to share?

A timid hand goes up, it's QUINCY TROUPE African American male 26, who stands up holding a paper in his hand.

> BUDD (CONT'D)
> Could you tell us your name?

> QUINCY TROUPE
> My name is Quincy. I don't have a
> name for my poem. It's something I
> just started working on.
>   (nervously reads)
> Ice sheets sweep this slick
> mirrored dark place space as keys
> that turn in tight, trigger pain of
> situations where we move ever so
> slowly, so gently, into time—traced
> agony the bright turning of
> imagination so slowly grooved
> through revolving doors, opening up
> to enter mountains where spirits
> walk voices, ever so slowly swept
> by cold, breathing fire...

All the Negro writers are hanging on every word when Quincy stops reading, looking embarrassed, he sits down.

> BUDD
> Quincy, please continue.

> QUINCY TROUPE
> Ah, I can't.

Alvin Saxon Jr. is sitting next to Quincy.

> ALVIN SAXON JR.
> Can I see that?

Quincy hands Alvin the paper he is holding. Alvin gently takes the paper from Quincy's hand and stands up and he eloquently reads from the paper.

> ALVIN SAXON JR. (CONT'D)
> ...As these elliptical moments of
> illusion link fragile loves sunk
> deep in snow as footprints, the
> voice prints cold black
> gesticulations bone bare, voices
> chewed skeletal choices in fangs of
> piranha gales spewing out slivers
> of raucous laughter glinting bright
> as hard polished silver nails.

EXT. WATTS - STREETS - DAY

Eric Priestley is being chased. He is frantically running from BLACK MAN #1, BLACK MAN #2, and BLACK MAN #3.

> BLACK MAN #1
> We gonna kill you nigga.

Eric's eyes are as big as quarters and he barely looks back.

> ERIC
> You gotta catch me first.

INT. WATTS - 9807 BEACH STREET - DAY

Budd sits at the head of the large group of Negro writers.

> BUDD
> OK, let's split into groups. Those
> interested in essays, short
> stories, and novels stay up front
> with me. Those interested in poems
> follow Johnie to the back.

> JOHNIE
> Alright, everybody follow me.

The Negro writers begin to separate into groups. It seems the older Negro writers work with Budd, and the younger Negro writers leave with Johnie. Among them is a tall and slender, ebony-skinned African American male named EMORY EVANS 20s.

> JOHNIE (CONT'D)
> Hey, Alvin. Emory is going to be
> staying here. Show him to his room
> and meet the rest of us in the
> backyard.

INT. WATTS - 9807 BEACH STREET - ROOM - DAY

Alvin walks in ahead of Emory.

> ALVIN SAXON JR.
> Well, this is it.

Emory looks around and sits on the bed.

> EMORY
> Ay, man, this is cool. It beats
> the street.

> ALVIN SAXON JR.
> So, what do you like to write?

> EMORY
> Romantic poetry. Emotional and
> soulful stuff.

> ALVIN SAXON JR.
> That's a contrast from the other
> young poets. All they want to
> write about is black militancy.
> Ay, man, I know a book you should
> check out. It's called "The
> Stranger," by Albert Camus. The
> story of an ordinary man
> unwittingly drawn into a senseless
> murder on an Algerian beach. It's
> a cool read.

> EMORY
> I'll have to check it out...

Suddenly Eric comes flying through the window like a missile
and lands on his back, flat on the floor.

Puzzled, Emory gazes down at the bruised and bloody Eric who
lies at his feet. Emory with a perfect British accent...

> EMORY (CONT'D)
> Eric, you are mad.

In the distance, the voice of Black Man #1 can be heard.

> BLACK MAN #1
> Tell that cat we gonna be right out
> here waiting on him.

INT. STUDIO WATTS - 103RD & GRANDEE AVENUE - DAY

The fingers of a bandaged hand play a few chords on the piano. Eric Priestley looking slightly bruised, a patch of gauze taped to his forehead, sits next to Alvin Saxon Jr.

                    ALVIN SAXON JR.
          Man, what was you thinking about?

                    ERIC
          Ojenke, I was thinking about
          survival.

                    ALVIN SAXON JR.
          You can't be bringing that kind of
          shit to the workshop.

                    ERIC
          That workshop has saved lives in
          more ways than one, namely mines.

                    ALVIN SAXON JR.
          Whatever you did, don't do it
          again. You may not be as lucky
          next time.

                    ERIC
          Yeah, you're right. -- Hey, man
          check this out.

Eric pulls a paper out of his back pocket.

                    ERIC (CONT'D)
          I've been working on this. It's
          called "Rain On The Mushroom." Let
          me know what you think.
               (reading)
          We sit & trapped walking balls of
          fat & sacks of water as the stain
          of retribution for the crime of
          poverty spreads the poison fang
          milkshake that strikes out flesh...

EXT. STUDIO WATTS - 103RD & GRANDEE AVENUE - DAY

Parked across the street is an army green van with a logo on it that reads *Maintenance Repair Service*.

INT. VAN - DAY

Wearing a maintenance jumpsuit, Michael Quinn headphones on his head, sits in front of a reel-to-reel tape recorder.

The door opens, and Brandon Cleary wearing a maintenance jumpsuit gets in holding a brown paper bag and two cans of sodas, he shuts the door.

                    BRANDON CLEARY
          What are they saying?

                    MICHAEL QUINN
          Care to take a listen?

Michael Quinn takes off the headphones holding them up to Brandon Cleary's ear. Eric Priestley's voice is heard coming out of the headphone speaker.

                    ERIC (V.O.)
          ...Down raw quick up loft no way
          plants sterile seeds & industry in
          junkyard time atomic clock through
          falling stock the telling numbers
          clutch the vanity of the thirsty
          rain no manufactured goods lost
          jobs new lifeblood us much CO-2...

Michael Quinn pulls back the headphones from Brandon Cleary's ear.

                    BRANDON CLEARY
          He's not making any sense.

                    MICHAEL QUINN
          He's a poet, poets don't need to
          make sense. It's a code.

                    BRANDON CLEARY
          A code?

                    MICHAEL QUINN
          Yeah, among orators, it's artistic
          communication. Didn't you learn
          anything during your FBI training?

                    BRANDON CLEARY
          Argh. I got two sandwiches, tuna
          fish and turkey. Which one do you
          want?

                    MICHAEL QUINN
          Tuna fish.

Brandon Cleary opens the brown paper bag and pulls out a sandwich, he hands it to Michael Quinn.

                    BRANDON CLEARY
          Here. You want the coke or the
          orange?

                    MICHAEL QUINN
          Coke.

Michael bites into the sandwich.

                    MICHAEL QUINN (CONT'D)
               (chewing)
          I think I want the turkey.

Brandon Cleary is about to bite into his sandwich.

                    BRANDON CLEARY
          C'mon, Quinn, focus on your job.

Michael puts on the headphones and turns to the reel-to-reel
tape recorder.

INT. STUDIO WATTS - 103RD & GRANDEE AVENUE - DAY

A young Negro artist sits a few feet from Eric and Alvin
drawing on a sketch pad.

Eric still sitting at the piano Alvin by his side plays
Brahms: Symphony No.2 in D major Op.73.

                    ERIC
          So what did you think?

                    ALVIN SAXON JR.
          Man, you're a complicated dude with
          a lot of talent.

                    ERIC
          Did you know we were born on the
          birthdays of Beethoven and Brahms,
          respectively?

                    ALVIN SAXON JR.
          Nah, I didn't know that.

The young Negro artist approaches Eric he stops playing. The
young Negro artist hands Eric the sketch pad. On the sketch
pad is a drawing depicting Eric and Alvin, reading poems with
musical notes coming out of their mouths instead of words;
the sketch is entitled "*Two Poets in Love with their people.*"

                    ERIC
          Aw, this is righteous.

Eric hands the sketch drawing to Alvin.

                    ALVIN SAXON JR.
          Man, this is beautiful. Thank,
          you.

INT. WATTS - 9807 BEACH STREET - EVENING

A raucous debate is going on between Johnie, Samuel, Jimmie,
Charles, and Sonora.

                    SAMUEL
          Nat Turner. He was known for the
          Southampton Insurrection. It's
          synonymous with the Watts
          rebellion.

                    JIMMIE
          Nah, nah, not that.

                    SAMUEL
          Then what?

                    JIMMIE
          Harriet Tubman.

                    CHARLES
          Nope, I like Norris Wright Cuney.

                    SAMUEL
          Man, don't nobody even know who
          that is?

                    CHARLES
          How bout Philip Alexander Bell?

                    SAMUEL
          Nah, not the cat that created the
          telephone.

                    JOHNIE
          Nah, Leumas, that was Alexander
          Graham Bell. Philip Alexander Bell
          was a newspaper editor and
          abolitionist.

                    SONORA MCKELLER
          I got it, everybody's gonna love
          this one. -- Frederick Douglass.
          Will call it, The Douglass House.

Johnie, Samuel, Jimmie, Charles, and Sonora look at each
other with a unanimous *Yeah!*

Budd walks in looking a bit concerned.

                    BUDD
          Is everything ok?

                    JOHNIE
          We've agreed on a name. The
          Douglass House.

                    BUDD
          I like it, that's perfect.

A loud belligerent hostile voice is heard coming from
outside.

                    BUDD (CONT'D)
          Now what's going on?

Harry Dolan comes rushing in.

                    BUDD (CONT'D)
          Who's making all that noise out
          there?

                    HARRY DOLAN
          It's David Moody, he's been
          drinking.

EXT. WATTS - 9807 BEACH STREET - FRONT YARD - EVENING

DAVID MOODY an African American male in his late 20s is
getting very aggressive as if he wants to fight two young
Negro males.

                    DAVID MOODY
          I will whoop both y'all asses. We
          all have to live here. Nobody
          gonna tell me what to do.

The two young Negro males look intimidated, they want no part
of David.

MILDRED WALTERS an African American female in her 20s steps
to David.

                    MILDRED WALTERS
          David why are you tripping, you
          need to cut out all that drinking.

                    DAVID MOODY
          Oh, cuz you my girl, you think you
          can tell me what to do?
                         (MORE)

                    DAVID MOODY (CONT'D)
          Take your ass in the house with the
          rest of them.

David pushes Mildred out of the way.

Just then Harry, Budd, Johnie, Samuel, Jimmie, Charles, and
Sanora come out.

                    HARRY DOLAN
          David, calm your ass down. You
          better listen to Mildred.

                    DAVID MOODY
          Oh, you want some of this too.

                    BUDD
          David, what's the problem? I'm
          sure we can work it out.

                    DAVID MOODY
          Everybody on my case. I'm too
          bossy. I act like a Sargent, I'm a
          bully. I'm the bad guy.

CLEVELAND SIMS a well-built African American male 26 steps
out of the crowd.

                    CLEVELAND SIMS
          Man, you look like a complete fool
          in front of everybody. You need to
          cut that shit out.

David get's up in Cleveland's personal space, they are nose-
to-nose and chest-to-chest.

                    DAVID MOODY
          Hey, dude, you're really pissing me
          off.

Cleveland chuckles, he's dismissive, not phased by David at
all.

                    CLEVELAND SIMS
          Well, David, that's unfortunate,
          but to be frank, I really don't
          give a shit, man.

                    DAVID MOODY
          Oh, yeah...

Budd is about to step in, but Harry quickly grabs him.

                    HARRY DOLAN
          Stay out of it Budd.

David backs away from Cleveland.

                    DAVID MOODY
          If you think you can do better,
          you're welcome to try.

Cleveland hee haws like a jackass, this angers David even
more.

                    CLEVELAND SIMS
          Dude, you're a very sorry fighter.
          My fourteen-year-old little sister
          could box your ears off.

                    DAVID MOODY
          Ok, ok...

David, head nodding, he's very jumpy.

                    DAVID MOODY (CONT'D)
          ...Then you should have no trouble
          big mouth, cause I'm gon put my two
          fists in it!

Cleveland chuckles to himself as he rolls up the sleeves of
his immaculate, well-pressed shirt.

                    CLEVELAND SIMS
          This is like getting tacos at a
          fiesta.

Cleveland squares off with David, who is bubbling with
confidence as he blurts out...

                    DAVID MOODY
          Yea nigga, I've been waiting to
          teach your snooty ass a lesson.

With their guards up, David and Cleveland, two strapping
young men warily circle each other.

                    DAVID MOODY (CONT'D)
                (taunting)
          Hey dude, don't get nervous, I
          won't make it too painful for your
          weak ass.

David throws a series of wind-producing left jabs, right
crosses, and uppercuts at the will-o-the-wispish Cleveland.

All of David's punches are way off the mark. Cleveland steps
away from David's hard and furious blows like a pro.

Cleveland bobs and weaves throwing his own rapid combinations, David looks like an old warrior who had kept fighting way past his prime.

Cleveland whips David hard. It's clear from the confident grin glued on Cleveland's face, that he enjoyed dishing out punishment to a well-chastened David.

A humbled David picks himself up off the ground assisted by Mildred.

>   MILDRED WALTERS
>   C'mon, baby. Let's go inside and
>   get you cleaned up.

EXT. ROCKEFELLER FOUNDATION BUILDING - DAY

Traffic traverses the street as the voice of Budd Schulberg is heard over city noise.

>   BUDD (V.O.)
>   I'm dealing with imminent budgetary
>   problems...

INT. ROCKEFELLER FOUNDATION - OFFICE - DAY

Budd looks troubled as he takes off his glasses and rubs his face.

Behind a desk sits NORMAN LLOYD a white male 58, he listens as Budd sitting in front of him opines.

>   BUDD
>   ...Estimated expenditures exceeded
>   revenues by nearly ninety-nine
>   thousand. I'm asking the
>   Rockefeller Foundation to consider
>   an annual funding commitment of one
>   hundred thousand.

Norman puts on his glasses and reviews some paper documents that lay in front of him.

>   NORMAN LLOYD
>   The arrival of proposed funds would
>   do little more than delay further
>   crises.

Norman studies a paper document.

                    NORMAN LLOYD (CONT'D)
          The budget estimates for nineteen
          sixty-eight show expected
          expenditures exceeding two hundred
          and fifty thousand.

Norman holds up a paper document directing it to Budd's
attention.

                    NORMAN LLOYD (CONT'D)
          This is confidential correspondence
          from the National Foundation for
          the Arts official Robert Walter,
          and the Rockefeller Foundation
          officials. Although you were
          encouraged to apply for two hundred
          and fifty thousand. It's unlikely
          that you will see such a large
          grant, and you might see as little
          as fifty thousand.

                    BUDD
          I can't operate The Douglass House
          on that.

                    NORMAN LLOYD
          You are seen as the sole force in
          Watts, working for the arts and
          Equal Opportunity, and your needs
          should be supported.

                    BUDD
          Then give me the money. Just stamp
          approved on my application.

                    NORMAN LLOYD
          Despite this favorable assessment,
          annual Rockefeller funding would
          come nowhere near that amount,
          instead hovering around the twenty-
          five thousand mark.

                    BUDD
          Argh, red tape in the way.

                    NORMAN LLOYD
          The conferral of tax-exempt status
          for the Douglass Foundation helps
          matters somewhat...

                    BUDD
          ...Between the National Endowment
          for the Arts, private donations,
          and grants from the Rockefeller and
          Randolph foundations, I'm still
          left short fifty-seven thousand
          dollars.

Norman takes off his glasses and reclines in his chair.

EXT. WATTS - 1690 EAST 103RD - DAY

A car pulls right up front of the burnt-out ruins of a
Safeway Supermarket building.

Budd gets out of the driver's side and Harry Dolan gets out
of the passenger side. They walk up and survey the remains
of the building.

                    BUDD
          Well, Harry, this is it. What do
          you think?

INT. WATTS - 1690 EAST 103RD - DAY

Budd and Harry walk around and observe the place stepping
over the charred debris.

                    BUDD
          We're expanding. This will be our
          new theater, and you'll be the
          director of theatrical development.

                    HARRY DOLAN
          Wow, Budd, I don't know what to
          say.

                    BUDD
          It doesn't look like much now.
          When construction is finished.
          There will be a stage, and this
          place will seat three hundred and
          fifty people.

Harry, smiles as he looks at the blackened skeletal remains
of what was once a supermarket.

EXT. WATTS - 9807 BEACH STREET - DAY

The premises are surrounded by Negroes clamoring to get in.
The heads and torsos are stuffed into windows, bodies are log
jammed at the front door entrance.

INT. WATTS - 9807 BEACH STREET - DAY

Budd and Harry sit at the head of a semi-circle that consists
of Johnie, Samuel, Jimmie, Charles, Sonora, Eric, Alvin,
Harley, and Fannie Brown.

AMIRI BARAKA African American male 33, sandwiched into a
window, with fire in his eyes, reads from a paper.

                    AMIRI BARAKA
          ...For all of him dead and gone and
          vanished from us, and all of him
          which clings to our speech black
          god of our time. For all of him,
          and all of yourself, look up, black
          man, quit stuttering and shuffling,
          look up, black man, quit whining
          and stooping, for all of him,
          For Great Malcolm a prince of the
          earth, let nothing in us rest until
          we avenge ourselves for his death,
          stupid animals that killed him, let
          us never breathe a pure breath if
          we fail, and white men call us
          faggots till the end of the earth.
          That's my poem, it's called, "A
          Poem for Black Hearts."

                    BUDD
          Thank you, Amiri, that was, ah, ah,
          very insightful.

A slender bushy haired wily looking African American male
OTIS O'SOLOMON 27, forces his way through the crowd at the
front door. He just starts reading from a paper.

                    OTIS O'SOLOMON
          An advocate of hate only with
          haters can relate, but, an advocate
          of Love, can communicate with the
          world and, since you must do, one
          of the two, why don't you do the
          best, LOVE, and bring respect into
          your life, and crown your soul with
          HAPPINESS. That's called "Love,"
          by Otis O'Solomon, that's me.

                    BUDD
          That was, yeah, ah, that was nice
          Otis. Are you considering joining
          the workshop?

                    OTIS O'SOLOMON
          I'd like to, but damn, I have to
          fight my way in here cuz it's so
          crowded.

Budd turns to Harry.

                    BUDD
               (whispers)
          I think we'll have to use the
          coffee house again. There's just
          not enough room here.

INT. BEVERLY HILLS CAFÉ - DAY

Seated at a sizeable table are ARABEL PORTER white female
40s, FREDERICKA WHITE, white female 30s, TED SIMMONS male
white 50s, DONNA CANNON white female 40s, JUANITA WATKINS
African American female 30s, and Adeline Schulberg.

Budd walks up carrying a stack of folders under his arm.

                    BUDD
          Hello, everyone, I'm sorry I'm
          late.

Budd sits the stack of folders on the table.

                    BUDD (CONT'D)
          Well, this is it.

                    ADELINE
          I know what my job is. But, who's
          going to be doing what?

                    BUDD
          I'm publishing eighteen writers.
          Nearly all of them have never been
          published before. We, Fredericka
          and I, are selecting those eighteen
          from approximately thirty
          contributors to the Watts Writers
          Workshop.

                    FREDERICKA
          I've been tracking down missing
          writers and their material.
          Assisting Budd in that area.

                    ARABEL
I'm the senior editor of The New
American Library. When Budd
called, I said I'd be glad to help.

                    BUDD
Ababel will work with Fredericka on
unusual editorial problems.

                    TED SIMMONS
So what do you need me to do?

                    BUDD
Ted is Deputy Director of the
Pacific Coast Writers' Conference
at Los Angeles State College. He's
been working with our Watts poet
circle. He will filter through
poems and other written material.

                    DONNA CANNON
What about me?

                    BUDD
Donna is a professional writer and
editor who enthusiastically
volunteered her time. I'll need
you to both screen and type a
profusion of manuscripts.

                    JUANITA WATKINS
And what assignment do you have for
me?

                    BUDD
Juanita, your help has been
invaluable to me and it's no
different in this case. You will
be doing a lot of typing. --
Mother thank you...

                    ADELINE
...He calls me Mother, everyone
else call me Ad, please.

                    BUDD
Ad waived her usual literary
agent's fee. And worked above and
beyond the call of agenting to
represent the economic interest of
the group.

The waiter brings a tray with food and drinks.

>   ADELINE
>   We took the liberty of ordering for
>   you.

>   BUDD
>   That's fine. It's a collective
>   effort.

INT. WATTS HAPPENING COFFEE HOUSE - EVENING

A hip-looking crowd of fashionable Negroes smoking cigarettes bob their heads to the music.

On a small stage, an ensemble band consisting of Horace Tapscott on piano, Stanley Crouch on the drums, and a couple of Negroes blowing on horns have a swing beat going. They are performing a hip jazzy toon titled *Seize The Time* performed by Elaine Brown.

>   ELAINE BROWN
>   (singing)
>   You tell me that the sun belongs to
>   you and should surround you but,
>   when I turn to look I see they've
>   snatched the sun from all around
>   you.

>   Why you hardly seem to want what's
>   yours, you hardly seem to care if
>   you love the sun, it's where you've
>   come from then you had better dare.

>   To Seize The Time The time is now
>   oh, Seize The Time, and you know
>   how.

>   You tell me that the soul is real,
>   and your soul must survive yet, I
>   see they've taken liberties with
>   your souls, and your lives.

>   Don't tell me that you lack
>   concern, for all that you must be,
>   'cause I know you know, you must
>   not be turned, and I know that you
>   can see.

>   To Seize The Time The time is now
>   oh, Seize The Time, and you know
>   how.

>   (MORE)

ELAINE BROWN (CONT'D)
You worry about liberty because
you've been denied well, I think
that you're mistaken or then, you
must have lied.

Cause you do not act like those who
care. You've never even fought for
the liberty you claim to lack, or
have you never thought?

To Seize The Time The time is now
oh, Seize The Time, and you know
how.

On the other side of the large space, Budd sits on a couch
surrounded by the usual group of Negro writers Harry, Johnie,
Samuel, Jimmie, Charles, Sonora, Eric, Alvin, Harley, and
Fannie Brown.

BUDD
I have a couple of announcements to
make. I combed through your
writing and poems and have compiled
them into collections that will be
published and released as a book.

The collective group gives off a jubilant reaction.

BUDD (CONT'D)
At least five workshop participants
are regularly writing for three
local television studios.

Elaine casually walks up.

ELAINE BROWN
Wow, he's back. The man that saved
the day. Mine if I sit down with
the group?

HARRY DOLAN
C'mon, Elaine, be cool.

JOHNIE
Everybody is welcome. Long as
you're not here to start no shit.

ELAINE BROWN
Nah man, It's cool, I'm here to
learn something. What can you
school me on Mr. Schulberg?

                    JOHNIE
          The workshop has filled an urgent
          need in an area where the senior
          high schools often lacked adequate
          speech and English departments.

                  ELAINE BROWN
          Score one for Schulberg.

Budd just looks on, he's unnerved.

                   HARRY DOLAN
          Whether criticized or praised,
          Schulberg's presence has shaped the
          fortunes of the Watts Writers
          Workshop.

                  ELAINE BROWN
          Score another one for Mr.
          Schulberg.

                    BUDD
          C'mon now, all of the cultural
          programs in Watts are here to work
          together.

                  ELAINE BROWN
              (sarcastic)
          You know what, you're right. I
          apologize, excuse me for
          interrupting.

                    BUDD
          The tv documentary The Angry Voices
          of Watts has been nominated for an
          Emmy award.

The group is elated and animated giving each other five, and
the black handshake.

Elaine sits there, moody, looking unimpressed.

                  BUDD (CONT'D)
          By the way, Elaine. I really like
          the song you performed.

                  ELAINE BROWN
          Maybe you can contact some of your
          Hollywood friends to donate money
          and help produce the album. It's
          called "Seize the Time," dedicated
          to the Black Panther Party.

Budd looks awkward, pursed lip, he rubs his brow.

EXT. STUDIO WATTS - 103RD & GRANDEE AVENUE - DAY

As pedestrians meander by and cars traverse the street the
rational voice of James Woods is heard.

                  JAMES (V.O.)
        What are you gonna do? Go over
        there and encourage a revolt.

INT. STUDIO WATTS - 103RD & GRANDEE AVENUE - DAY

In the background, a group of Negro sculptures work on pieces
of art.

James is confronted by ANTHONY AMDE HAMILTON African American
male 21, RICHARD DEDEAUX African American male 27, and Otis
O'Solomon.

                  JAMES
        I, mean, Schulberg ain't my
        favorite person, but I don't wanna
        take down his workshop.

                  AMDE
        That's not what I'm trying to do.
        That's where I got started. I
        learned a lot from Schulberg. But
        I'm forming my own group.

                  JAMES
            (to Richard)
        What about you? You gonna go over
        and recruit poets from Schulberg's
        workshop?

                RICHARD DEDEAUX
        I'm with Amde. We're gonna spread
        the word. If poets from the Watts
        Writers Workshop defect, so be it.

                  JAMES
            (to Otis)
        And you?

               OTIS O'SOLOMON
        I'm leaving because of "subtle
        censorship" and "literary
        sharecropping." It's a divide
        between the older, more politically
        moderate, and the young blacks that
        have radical ideals.

                    JAMES
What you gonna call yourselves?

                    AMDE
The Watts Thirteen.

                    JAMES
Wow, sound like cats that escaped
from the pen.

                    AMDE
That's how we feel. We have to
express that in our spoken word.

                    JAMES
You ought to think about a
different name.

                    AMDE
We'll see.

                    JAMES
Well, you're always welcome here at
Studio Watts.

                    AMDE
I appreciate that brotha, thanks.

EXT. WATTS - 9807 BEACH STREET - BACKYARD - DAY

Johnie, Samuel, Alvin, Eric, and several other young Negroes
are carousing together. Cups in there hands, Johnie is
pouring shots of liquor.

                    JOHNIE
It's party time, everybody drink
up.

                    ERIC
          (sips and frowns)
Pugh, where's the ice?

                    JOHNIE
That's cognac. That shit is
smooth, don't need any ice.

                    ALVIN SAXON JR.
You have to drink it slowly.

                    ERIC
You shoulda at least got something
to cut it with.

                    SAMUEL
          You ain't got no beer.

                    JOHNIE
          For what.
               (holds up liquor bottle)
          This is all we need.

Johnie reaches into his pocket and pulls out a plastic bag
containing red devils.

                    JOHNIE (CONT'D)
          Who's ready for some of this?

Johnie dangles the plastic bag.

Budd looks out of the window of the house, he watches as
Johnie passes around red devils.

Johnie, Samuel, Alvin, Eric, and the other young Negroes pop
the pills and chase them with gulps of liquor.

Budd walks out of the back door and approaches Johnie,
Samuel, Alvin, Eric, and the other young Negroes.

                    JOHNIE (CONT'D)
          Ay, y'all there he is.

                    BUDD
               (casual)
          Hey, guys, what's going on?

                    JOHNIE
               (high)
          C'mon, Budd. Have a drink with us.

                    SAMUEL
          Yeah, Budd, here take a sip.

Samuel holds his cup out to Budd.

                    BUDD
          No, thanks, Leumas.

                    ERIC
               (high)
          Budd you need to have a drink
          sometime, and it doesn't have to be
          over dinner.

                    BUDD
          You're right, but I'll pass all the
          same.

                    ALVIN SAXON JR.
          You're gonna have to drink with us
          at some point.

                    BUDD
          I promise I'll have a drink with
          you guys, and It'll be on me. --
          Johnie can I talk to you for a
          minute?

Budd and Johnie step out of earshot.

                    BUDD (CONT'D)
          Look, Johnie, you're one of the
          leaders of the workshop. You
          should watch it with the pills.

                    JOHNIE
          Don't worry, I have it under
          control, believe me.

                    BUDD
          I hope so, you're future is bright.
          You don't want to mess that up.

                    JOHNIE
          I hear you loud and clear.

Budd pulls out an envelope and hands it to Johnie.

                    BUDD
          It's from Stanford.

Johnie lights up and opens the envelope and pulls out a
letter.

                    JOHNIE
                (reading)
          Aw, got damn. I've been accepted.
          I secured a fellowship at Stanford.

Johnie turns to Samuel, Alvin, Eric, and the other young
Negroes. He holds up the acceptance letter.

                    JOHNIE (CONT'D)
          Ay, y'all, I'm in. I've been
          accepted to Stanford University.

Samuel, Alvin, Eric, and the other young Negroes raise their
cups to Johnie.

High, Johnie turns back to Budd.

                    JOHNIE (CONT'D)
          Budd, I don't know what to say.
          Thanks, man, thank you.

INT. WATTS - 9807 BEACH STREET - DAY

Harry Dolan sits in front of David Moody, Mildred Walters,
Charles Johnson, Cleveland Sims, and Emory Evans. A few
other Negroes sit amongst the group.

                    HARRY DOLAN
          The workshop has seen growth right
          from the outset. It's continually
          evolving. That's why I'm happy to
          let y'all know about a new phase
          the Douglass House is undertaking.
          -- Um, Um, anybody curious as to
          what that is?

                    CHARLES
          I'm, sure you'll tell us.

                    SONORA MCKELLER
          C'mon, man, stop beating around the
          bush.

                    HARRY DOLAN
          Alright. We will be hosting
          courses in screenplay writing,
          acting, television and film
          editing, motion picture camera
          operation, and film production.

                    EMORY
          Sounds like we're turning into a
          full fledge studio.

                    CLEVELAND SIMS
          That's cool, man, cuz a lot of us
          want to act.

                    HARRY DOLAN
          I've written a play. It's called
          "Big Time Buck White," and David, I
          want you to play the lead.

David lights up, he's ecstatic, and so is Mildred.

                    MILDRED WALTERS
          You hear that, baby.

                    DAVID MOODY
          Aw, man, wow. Thanks, Harry.

                    HARRY DOLAN
          I'll need everyone's help. Budd
          purchased the Safeway Supermarket
          that was burnt down in the riot.

                    CHARLES
          Uprising.

                    HARRY DOLAN
          Right. -- It's being converted
          into a theater. So I'll need
          volunteers to help clear out all
          the trash and debris.

A hand goes up and catches Harry's attention, he squints at
the person.

                    HARRY DOLAN (CONT'D)
          Yeah, brotha, you have a question?
          You don't look familiar, you must
          be new to the workshop.

It's DARTHARD PERRY alias Ed Riggs African American male 20,
revolutionary in his appearance and militant persona. Perry
dragging on a Pall Mall cigarette stands up from his seat.

                    DARTHARD PERRY
          You mentioned television and film
          editing. That's an area I'd like
          to be involved with. I'm a student
          at L.A.C.C., I'm studying
          television production.

                    HARRY DOLAN
          What's your name brotha?

                    DARTHARD PERRY
          Ed, Ed Riggs.

                    HARRY DOLAN
          Ed, when I came to the workshop.
          The first assignment I got was
          janitor. If you don't have a
          problem using a mop and vacuum,
          you're welcome here.

                    DARTHARD PERRY
          When do I start?

                    HARRY DOLAN
          That attitude will take you far.

INT. HOME OF BUDD SCHULBERG - LIVING ROOM - EVENING

Budd walks in and is greeted by Geraldine.

> GERALDINE
> (kisses Budd on the lips)
> Hey sweetheart, how'd it go today?

Budd and Geraldine sit down on the couch.

> BUDD
> It's always a challenge, but the
> opportunities that have opened up
> for the group outweigh any
> obstacles that come up. -- I'm
> sorry, I'm so consumed with the
> workshop, we haven't had time to
> catch up.

> GERALDINE
> Well, my agent sent me on some
> auditions. I hope to book at least
> one of the parts.

> BUDD
> You will.

> GERALDINE
> So what's next for the workshop?

> BUDD
> The Department of Health,
> Education, and Welfare has
> contracted the Douglass House to
> write pamphlets with the stated
> purpose of explaining programs in
> terms, "people in ghetto
> communities can understand."

> GERALDINE
> Oh, that's great.

> BUDD
> Of course, there's the theater,
> it's under renovation.

> GERALDINE
> Have you thought of a name?

> BUDD
> Yeah, the Douglass Theater. I'll
> have to run it by the group.

>   GERALDINE
> Nice. Look how far you've come in
> three years. Who woulda imagined?

>   BUDD
> Yeah. You know, I'm thinking of
> asking Bobby to speak to the group.

>   GERALDINE
> Ooh, wonderful. Do you think he'll
> do it?

>   BUDD
> I hope so.

INT. WATTS - 1690 EAST 103RD - DAY

The sound of hammers banging in concert with that of circular
saws cutting wood makes for its own melody.

Construction workers carry plywood and lumber. The drywall
is being hoisted up on scaffolding.

Darthard Perry alias Ed Riggs is wearing jeans construction
boots, and a long sleeve plaid shirt hammers nails into
plywood in what looks to be a stage.

David Moody and Cleveland Sims walk up holding a push broom
and dustpans.

>   DAVID MOODY
> Ay, Ed, man, be cool with that
> hammer.

>   CLEVELAND SIMS
> Yeah, you'll be no good with a
> busted thumb.

Perry takes a nail from his mouth and hammers away at the
plywood.

>   DARTHARD PERRY
> When I'm finished with this stage
> it's gonna be looking good.

Harry Dolan walks up wearing slacks and a button-down shirt.

>   HARRY DOLAN
> Everything is coming together.
>   (looking at David and
>   Cleveland)
> You cats alright? Is everything
> cool?

                    CLEVELAND SIMS
          Yeah, man, we're cool.

                    DAVID MOODY
          I'm saving my performance for the
          stage.

Mildred Walters and Emory Evans walk up carrying paint
rollers and wearing overalls with blotches of paint on them.

                    MILDRED WALTERS
                (to David)
          Hey, baby, you wanna trade places
          with me?

                    DAVID MOODY
          Nah, I'll stick with picking up
          trash.

                    EMORY
          Man, I can't believe how fast
          things are coming together.

                    HARRY DOLAN
          We open in a month. Man, can you
          believe it? I use to buy my
          groceries in this place.

Harry gazes at all of the construction going on around him.

EXT. CAR - STREET - DAY

Brandon Cleary sits in the driver's seat, he is unwrapping a
sandwich.

Michael Quinn sitting in the passenger seat bites into a
sandwich, an odd look dawns on his face, he stops chewing and
stares at Brandon Cleary.

Brandon Cleary bites into his sandwich, chewing vigorously he
notices Michael Quinn staring at him, and he stops chewing.

                    BRANDON CLEARY
          What now?

                    MICHAEL QUINN
          My sandwich has mayonnaise on it.
                (annoyed)
          A Pastrami should not have
          mayonnaise on it.

                    BRANDON CLEARY
          What is it with you and these
          sandwiches?

                    MICHAEL QUINN
          What kind of sandwich do you have?

                    BRANDON CLEARY
          Reuben.

                    MICHAEL QUINN
          What kind of dressing is on it?

Brandon takes a bite out of the sandwich, chewing...

                    BRANDON CLEARY
          Tangy Russian dressing.

                    MICHAEL QUINN
          Tangy Russian.

                    BRANDON CLEARY
          Yeah.

                    MICHAEL QUINN
          When you ordered my Pastrami. Why
          didn't you just say, put mustard on
          it?

                    BRANDON CLEARY
          Didn't think about it.

A phone *rings* from a nearby phone booth.

                    BRANDON CLEARY (CONT'D)
               (chewing)
          That's him.

EXT. CAR - STREET - DAY

The car door opens, and Michael Quinn scrambles out he races
over to the phone booth.

INT. PHONE BOOTH - DAY

Michael Quinn quickly picks up the phone.

                    MICHAEL QUINN
          Hello. -- Yeah, what'd you find
          out. Do they suspect anything? --
          Good. -- OK, just report back to
          me.

INT. WATTS HAPPENING COFFEE HOUSE - DAY

Angry grumblings are coming from a crowd of Negroes.

In the audience are Samuel "Leumas Sirrah" Harris, Johnie
Scott, Charles Johnson, Eric Priestley, Jimmie Sherman,
Fannie Carole Brown, Harley Mims, Sonora McKeller, Quincy
Troupe, Emory Evans, Alvin "Ojenke" Saxon Jr., David Moody,
Mildred Walters, Cleveland Sims, Otis O'Solomon, Anthony
"Amde" Hamilton, Richard Dedeaux, Amiri Baraka, and Darthard
Perry.

Samuel shouts from his chair.

                    SAMUEL
          If you call it a riot, it sounds
          like it was just a bunch of crazy
          people who went out and did bad
          things for no reason. I maintain
          it was somewhat understandable, if
          not acceptable. So I call it a
          rebellion.

Alvin shouts from his chair.

                    ALVIN SAXON JR.
          Riots are the voices of the
          unheard.

On the small stage is Robert F. Kennedy. Standing on either
side of Robert F. Kennedy are Budd Schulberg and Harry Dolan.

                    ROBERT F. KENNEDY
          I can't say I completely
          understand. No wrongs have ever
          been righted by riots and civil
          disorders...

Also in the audience are James Wood, Elaine Brown, Horace
Tapscott, and Stanley Crouch.

                    ELAINE BROWN
          Aw, that's bullshit man. You're
          just here to gain votes.

                    ROBERT F. KENNEDY
          An uncontrolled or uncontrollable
          mob is only the voice of madness.

Amde shouts from his chair.

                    AMDE
          Man, you sound just like the Feds.

Charles Johnson shouts from his chair.

                    CHARLES
          C'mon, give the man a chance.

                    ROBERT F. KENNEDY
          There's a lot of tension in here.
          I will say this, I fully support
          the anti-poverty cultural programs
          of Watts. Everyone in here is a
          light, a bright light of change.
          Let your anger fuel change, be a
          voice of reason. -- Don't act
          rashly, but be rational-minded, and
          you will ultimately discover a
          change in your community.

Robert F. Kennedy is met with a mixed round of applause.

EXT. WATTS HAPPENING COFFEE HOUSE - DAY

Surrounded by a cadre of secret service men. Budd and Robert
F. Kennedy walk out and stand next to a limousine.

                    BUDD
          They were pretty rough on you.

                    ROBERT F. KENNEDY
          We're only a few years removed from
          the riots. So there is a lot of
          resentment toward the government
          and the police.

                    BUDD
          The Douglass Theater opens in a
          month...

                    ROBERT F. KENNEDY
          ...Don't Worry, whatever I can do
          to support you and the people of
          Watts.

Budd and Robert F. Kennedy shake hands. Robert F. Kennedy is
ushered into the limousine. The secret service men get into
a car, and the caravan pulls off.

INT. WATTS - 9807 BEACH STREET - DAY

The vibrating blare from a vacuum cleaner is heard. Darthard
Perry thoroughly pushes and pulls a vacuum over the carpet.

Budd walks in holding a book, he is greeted by Harry Dolan who holds a paper in his hand.

> BUDD
> It just arrived.

> HARRY DOLAN
> Huh?

> BUDD
> The book, it just arrived.

> HARRY DOLAN
> Wait a minute...

Harry turns to Darthard Perry alias Ed Riggs, raising his voice.

> HARRY DOLAN (CONT'D)
> ...Ay Ed, turn off that vacuum.

Darthard hits a switch on the Vacuum and it goes silent.

Budd holds the book out to Harry, he takes it and his face lights up with excitement.

> HARRY DOLAN (CONT'D)
> Man, "From The Ashes: Voices of
> Watts."

Harry opens the book scanning through it.

> HARRY DOLAN (CONT'D)
> "I Remember Papa," "Will There Be
> Another Riot in Watts," "The Sand-
> Clock Day," "Crazy Nigger, Losers
> Weepers." Wow, I don't know what
> to say.

Budd beams with pride as he looks at Harry.

> BUDD
> I'm thankful to have a part in all
> the writers, whose works, are
> published in the book.

Darthard Perry steps up.

> DARTHARD PERRY
> Can I see that?

> HARRY DOLAN
> Sure.

Harry hands Darthard alias Ed Riggs the book, he eyes the cover.

>   DARTHARD PERRY
> You're in here?

>   HARRY DOLAN
> Yep, I am. -- Budd this is Ed
> Riggs. He'll be working in the TV
> department once the theater opens.

>   BUDD
> Nice to meet you Ed.

Darthard huge smile on his face, still looking at the book cover.

>   DARTHARD PERRY
> "Edited with an introduction by
> Budd Schulberg." Man, wow, now I
> know I've landed in the right
> place.

Harry, looks at the paper in his hand, he frowns and hands it to Budd.

>   BUDD
> Huh...
>   (reads)
> Watts Poets. A new organization
> explicitly dedicated to "fostering
> positive black imagery." Those
> interested in joining contact Amde.

>   HARRY DOLAN
> He's been circulating the flyer to
> all the cultural programs. Some of
> the writers are leaving to work
> with Amde.

>   BUDD
> Argh. Well, I figure something
> like this would eventually happen.

Darthard Perry, smirks and looks at Budd and Harry, turns on the Vacuum, and begins pushing and pulling over the carpet.

INT. L.A. FEDERAL BUREAU OF INVESTIGATION - OFFICE - DAY

Will Heaton sits on the edge of his desk.

>   WILL HEATON
> Has Othello gained excess?

Brandon Cleary and Michael Quinn are sitting in front of Will Heaton.

                    BRANDON CLEARY
          He has.

                    WILL HEATON
          Is he feeding you information that
          can help us?

Michael Quinn looks at his notes.

                    MICHAEL QUINN
          A new revolutionary group is trying
          to take root. They call themselves
          the Watts Prophets.

                    WILL HEATON
          Hoover wrote an internal memorandum
          to all FBI offices. The purpose of
          this new counterintelligence
          endeavor is to expose, disrupt,
          misdirect, discredit, or otherwise
          neutralize the activities of black
          nationalist hate-type organizations
          and groupings, their leadership,
          spokesmen, membership, and
          supporters. You have to keep the
          pressure on Othello.

                    BRANDON CLEARY
          So far he has access to all the
          cultural programs. Watts Writers
          Workshop is the most relevant.

                    WILL HEATON
          If we take them down, that will
          create a domino effect, the rest
          will fall.

EXT. WATTS - 1690 EAST 103RD - DAY

The roll-up doors of a bobtail truck open, and inside are
cameras, audio, lighting, and editing equipment.

As the tailgate drops, Darthard, Johnie, and Jimmie begin
unloading the equipment.

INT. WATTS - 1690 EAST 103RD - DAY

Budd and Harry watch as Darthard, Johnie, and Jimmie haul in
the cameras, audio, lighting, and editing equipment.

                    HARRY DOLAN
          Sit everything over there in the
          corner for now.

As Johnie and Darthard carefully situate a camera.

                    JOHNIE
          Ay, man, you should be over here
          helping us.

                    HARRY DOLAN
          Somebody gotta supervise.

Darthard Perry walks up smoking a Pall Mall cigarette.

                    DARTHARD PERRY
          Wow, this is some top-of-the-line
          production equipment.

                    BUDD
          We have NBC to thank, they donated
          all the equipment.

                    DARTHARD PERRY
              (to Harry)
          So, I'm being promoted from janitor
          to production supervisor?

                    HARRY DOLAN
          That's a big responsibility.

                    DARTHARD PERRY
          I can handle it.

                    HARRY DOLAN
          OK. We'll see. You screw up and
          you'll be demoted back to a
          janitor.

                    BUDD
          Bobby is coming to the opening. He
          wants a tour of the theater.

                    DARTHARD PERRY
          What!

                    HARRY DOLAN
          Nah, bullshit.

                    BUDD
          The press will be here. He's going
          to make a speech. They'll be a
          huge crowd out front.

                    HARRY DOLAN
          Man, Watts will definitely be
          buzzing.

EXT. WATTS - HOUSE - MORNING

The place looks quaint and modest, children horseplay as they
walk past carrying school books.

INT. WATTS - HOUSE - ROOM - MORNING

Laying in bed, a sleeping prostrate naked NEGRO WOMAN rests
her head on Darthard Perry's chest. With one arm behind his
head, Perry's eyes are wide open, he reaches over to a
nightstand and picks up a watch.

Checking the time on the watch, Perry slips from under the
naked Negro woman and sits up on the edge of the bed. He
then grabs the phone from the nightstand and begins to dial.

                    DARTHARD PERRY
          -- Yeah, it's me. Right, this
          afternoon. Yeah, he'll be there.
          Both of'em will be there. -- OK.

Perry hangs up the phone, and the naked Negro woman is roused
out of her sleep.

                    NEGRO WOMAN
          Who was that?

Perry with a slight turn of the head.

                    DARTHARD PERRY
          Nobody important.

                    NEGRO WOMAN
          Baby.

                    DARTHARD PERRY
          Yeah.

                    NEGRO WOMAN
          -- I think I'm pregnant.

Perry, silent, turns looking straight ahead.

                    NEGRO WOMAN (CONT'D)
          Did you hear me?

                    DARTHARD PERRY
          Yeah, I heard you.

EXT. WATTS - 1690 EAST 103RD - PARKING LOT - DAY

A banner hangs on the wall of the building that reads *Watts Writers Workshop Welcomes Robert F. Kennedy*.

Signs bob up and down that read *Kennedy for President*.

Throngs of Negroes young and old are crowded around a stage. Cameramen and the reporters jostle for position.

On the stage, Robert F. Kennedy stands at the microphone looking out at the crowd.

> ROBERT F. KENNEDY
> What we need in the United States
> is not division; what we need in
> the United States is not hatred;
> what we need in the United States
> is not violence or lawlessness, but
> is love and wisdom, and compassion
> toward one another, and a feeling
> of justice towards those who still
> suffer within our country, whether
> they be white or whether they be
> black.

The crowd that is overwhelmingly Negro cheer and applaud.

Wearing press credentials, Brandon Cleary and Michael Quinn sift through the crowd.

> ROBERT F. KENNEDY (CONT'D)
> I believe that the country needs
> and wants unity between blacks and
> whites. I encourage the country to
> dedicate ourselves to what the
> Greeks wrote so many years ago: "to
> tame the savageness of man and to
> make gentle the life of this
> world."

The crowd responds enthusiastically with more cheers and applause.

> ROBERT F. KENNEDY (CONT'D)
> Lastly, I would say to the people
> of Watts and to the country at
> large. Pray for our country and
> for our people. It's not about me,
> It's about us! We can do this
> together. Thank you.

The crowd explodes in applause and enthusiasm.

INT. WATTS - 1690 EAST 103RD - DAY

Accompanied by secret service men, Budd and Robert F. Kennedy
tour the theater.

                    BUDD
          It seats three hundred and fifty
          people. Over there is the control
          room. We have cameras set up
          around the stage. We have lighting
          as you can see, and audio recording
          equipment.

                    ROBERT F. KENNEDY
          Budd, this is really special. Your
          workshop is the cultural hub of
          Watts.

                    BUDD
          I had a lot of help from donors
          like yourself.

                    ROBERT F. KENNEDY
          It's a worthy cause. -- I'm giving
          a speech this evening at the
          Ambassador Hotel. I want you to be
          there.

                    BUDD
          Of course.

Budd and Robert F. Kennedy, with secret service men in tow
continue to walk about the theater.

EXT. AMBASSADOR HOTEL - EVENING

The place is bustling with activity.

Cars pull up in the front, and valets jump into cars and park
them.

INT. AMBASSADOR HOTEL - ROOM - EVENING

Robert F. Kennedy is sitting on the floor he looks to be in a
peculiar state.

The door opens, and Robert F. Kennedy's CAMPAIGN MANAGER and
Budd Schulberg walk in. The Campaign Manager stops in his
tracks, he looks confused.

                    CAMPAIGN MANAGER
          Robert, why are you sitting on the
          floor? We have to get downstairs.

Robert F. Kennedy shakes himself and slowly gets up from the
floor.

Budd gawks at Kennedy...

                    BUDD
          Bobby, are you ok?

                    ROBERT F. KENNEDY
          Yeah, um, I'm fine. I'm fine. --
          Look Budd, If I'm elected
          President. I'm going to implement
          the Watts Writers Workshop format
          on a national level. All over the
          country.

                    BUDD
          I don't know what to say.

                    CAMPAIGN MANAGER
          Robert, let's go. We have to get
          down to the ballroom.

INT. AMBASSADOR HOTEL - HALLWAY - CONTINUOUS

The room door opens Robert F. Kennedy briskly walks out
followed by Budd and the Campaign Manager.

INT. AMBASSADOR HOTEL - BALLROOM - CONTINUOUS

In front of a packed raucous crowd waving campaign signs,
Robert F. Kennedy stands at the podium. A few feet from
Kennedy stands Budd.

                    ROBERT F. KENNEDY
          I would hope, I would hope, now
          that the California primary is
          finished. Now that these primaries
          are over. That we can now
          concentrate on having a dialogue,
          or a debate, I hope. Between the
          vice president and perhaps myself
          on what direction we want to go in
          the United States.

The crowd cheers.

                    ROBERT F. KENNEDY (CONT'D)
          What we're going to do in the rural
          areas of our country? What we're
          going to do for those who still
          suffer within the United States
          from hunger? What were going to do
          around the rest of the globe and
          whether were going to continue the
          policies that have been so
          unsuccessful? In Vietnam, American
          Troops and American Marines carried
          the major burden of that conflict.
          We can not continue with failed
          policies, and I think we should
          move in a different direction.

More whistles and cheers come from the crowd.

                    ROBERT F. KENNEDY (CONT'D)
          So, so I thank all of you who made
          this possible this evening. All of
          the effort that you made, and all
          the people's names I haven't
          mentioned. But did all the work at
          the precinct level. Who got out
          the vote, who did all of the
          effort, ah, brought forth all the
          effort that's required. Thank you
          and good night.

The crowd gives a resounding round of applause and gleeful
cheers.

Robert F. Kennedy exits the stage along with the Campaign
Manager, Budd, and an entourage of people.

INT. AMBASSADOR HOTEL - KITCHEN - CONTINUOUS

Cooks and dishwashers are fast at work when Robert F. Kennedy
is ushered through by secret service men, the Campaign
Manager, Budd, and an entourage of well-wishers.

From seemingly out of nowhere SIRHAN SIRHAN a 5'5" 24-year-
old Jordanian appears. Pointing a gun that can be construed
as a toy pistol, Sirhan Sirhan shoots Kennedy.

Chaos ensues, people are screaming and shouting.

The secret service men immediately subdue Sirhan Sirhan and
wrest the gun from him.

Budd is stunned, his mouth agape, he looks on as Robert F.
Kennedy lies on the floor mortally wounded.

INT. HOME OF BUDD SCHULBERG - LIVING ROOM - DAY

Standing in front of the television sobbing is Geraldine.

On the television screen is a Caucasian man, FRANK
MANKIEWICZ, a caption on the television screen reads *LIVE
GOOD SAMARITAN HOSPITAL.*

>   FRANK MANKIEWICZ
>   Senator Robert Francis Kennedy died
>   at one forty-four AM today, June
>   sixth nineteen sixty-eight. With
>   Senator Kennedy at the time of his
>   death -- Were his wife Ethel, his
>   sister Mrs. Steven Smith, Miss
>   Patricia Lawford, brother in Law
>   Mr. Steven Smith, his sister-in-law
>   Misses John F. Kennedy.

A caption on the television screen reads *FRANK MANKIEWICZ
KENNEDY PRESS SECRETARY.*

>   FRANK MANKIEWICZ (CONT'D)
>   He was, uh, forty-two years old.
>   Thank you.

On the television screen, Frank Mankiewicz depressed
demeanor, walks away from the microphone-laden lectern.

The sound of the front door opening is heard, and Budd walks
in.

Geraldine rushes up to Budd they hug tightly as she cries.
Budd helps Geraldine to the couch, they sit down.

Tears in her eyes Geraldine looks at Budd.

>   GERALDINE
>   What are we gonna do?

Budd takes a deep breath, long face, and looks at Geraldine.

>   BUDD
>   What else can we do but continue
>   on?

>   GERALDINE
>   First, John, then Martin, now this.
>   It all seems so hopeless.

Budd stands up from the couch his shoulders slouched as
Geraldine looks up at him.

> BUDD
> You can never give up hope. That's
> all we have.

EXT. WATTS - 1690 EAST 103RD - EVENING

A large marquee sits adjacent to the parking lot, it reads
*Douglass Watts Writers Theater Harry Dolan Presents Big Time
Buck White*.

Accompanied by *gospel music, tambourines shaking, applause,
and a cacophony of spirited voices*. The crooning voice of
David Moody is heard.

> DAVID MOODY (V.O.)
> We came in chains. We didn't
> volunteer...

INT. WATTS - 1690 EAST 103RD - STAGE - EVENING

Standing at a raised lectern with a microphone attached to it
is David Moody. He has on a huge afro wig, a fake full
beard, and a Moses-esque long shawl.

David is surrounded by ten Negroes dressed in hip 1960s
attire with raised black power fists high in the air.

> DAVID MOODY
> (crooning to gospel music)
> ...And yet today the fact remains
> we're still held captive here. We
> came in chains. Now we say cut us
> loose. Though that may go against
> your grain, still there's no
> excuse. We came in chains...

The ten Negroes like agitated protesters clamor adamantly.

> DAVID MOODY (CONT'D)
> ...Now who will bear the cost.
> Till every one of us regains the
> freedom we have lost. We came in
> chains. Now your choice must be,
> to either blow out all our brains
> or else just set us free!

The ten Negroes in unison shout out *FREE!*

INT. WATTS - 1690 EAST 103RD - CONTROL ROOM - CONTINUOUS

Darthard Perry alias Ed Riggs, with headphones on, looks at
David Moody's performance through the plexiglass window as he
tweaks the controls of an audio tape recorder.

INT. WATTS - 1690 EAST 103RD - STAGE - CONTINUOUS

David Moody still standing at the raised lectern with a
microphone attached to it, is giving an animated performance.

>   DAVID MOODY
>   ...Chains, we came in chains, four
>   hundred years, no justice, no
>   freedom, no equality...

The ten Negroes excitedly chant and howl while raising
rattling chains high in the air.

>   DAVID MOODY (CONT'D)
>   ...Working from sun up till
>   sundown, nineteen seventy, still in
>   chains. Financial chains,
>   economical chains. Chains, chains,
>   chains...

The ten Negroes writhe about hoisting chains, letting out
feverish chilling howls.

Trumpets from the gospel track blare loudly.

>   DAVID MOODY (CONT'D)
>   America! Chains, chains, chains,
>   chains...

There's a drum roll, more chants, and howls from the ten
Negroes. Raucous sounds and music fade down.

The audience applauds with vigor, they stand up from their
seats.

David Moody and the ten Negro actors line up together and
take a bow.

INT. WATTS - 1690 EAST 103RD - BACKSTAGE - CONTINUOUS

A jubilant Harry Dolan greets David Moody they slap five.

>   HARRY DOLAN
>   Man, you got down brotha.

                    DAVID MOODY
          I was nervous, but I got through
          it.

Budd walks up with a bright smile.

                    BUDD
          David, you were tremendous. Did
          you see the reaction of the crowd?

                    DAVID MOODY
          Man, did I.

                    BUDD
          Congratulations Harry. You did a
          wonderful job.

                    HARRY DOLAN
          Thanks, Budd. I really appreciate
          that.

INT. ROCKEFELLER FOUNDATION - OFFICE - DAY

A frustrated-looking Budd Schulberg sits in front of Norman
Lloyd.

                    NORMAN LLOYD
          Look, Budd, I didn't want to drag
          you in here like this. Foundation
          funds are limited. I hoped that a
          closer working relationship between
          the Watts Writers Workshop, Studio
          Watts, and the Watts Happening
          Coffee House might be forged.

                    BUDD
          I'm puzzled by the seeming lack of
          interest in greater cooperation
          myself.

                    NORMAN LLOYD
          The fact you're moving to New York
          doesn't help. Philanthropic
          organizations, government
          officials, public and private
          donors, might well have continued
          to prioritize the Watts Writers
          Workshop.

                    BUDD
          Why does everything have to hinge
          on me? Harry Dolan is running the
          workshop now.

              NORMAN LLOYD
Harry's a fine choice, but he's not
Budd Schulberg.

              BUDD
I need you to support him, and
continue to support the workshop.

              NORMAN LLOYD
Budd, I'm going to be straight with
you. The civil unrest that ensued
after King's assassination. The
well-publicized feuding between the
Black Panther Party and the US
Organization. Budgetary problems
extend well beyond Watts, as
national affairs increasingly seem
to suggest, five years of concerted
anti-poverty funding has
accomplished little. As a result,
the Rockefeller Foundation is
temporarily suspending funding for
Equal Opportunity programs.

Looking dumbfounded, Budd just sits there, his silent
response speaks volumes.

INT. WATTS - 1690 EAST 103RD - LOBBY - DAY

A trophy case displays numerous accolades honoring the Watts
Writers Workshop. Standing out prominently is an *Emmy Award*.

Budd and Harry walk up gazing at the awards in the display
case.

              BUDD
Harry, you know, as the saying
goes, "You can't rest on your
laurels."

              HARRY DOLAN
That's what they say.

              BUDD
It happens to be true.
    (somber look)
I wanted you to meet me here
because I wanted to tell you first.

              HARRY DOLAN
Are you ok? I don't like where
this is going.

                    BUDD
          I'm moving to New York.
          Permanently.

                    HARRY DOLAN
          Wow. That's a punch in the gut.

                    BUDD
          And... The Rockefeller Foundation
          and the National Foundation for the
          Arts have cut off their support.

                    HARRY DOLAN
          Why? I don't understand.

                    BUDD
          I don't either, but that's the
          reality.

                    HARRY DOLAN
          What about the workshop? What are
          we gonna do without you?

                    BUDD
          You're going to continue to run
          things. I'm going to start another
          workshop, which will be affiliated
          with the Douglass House.

                    HARRY DOLAN
          That's, heavy man. You just laid
          some heavy shit on me.

                    BUDD
          You can handle it. That's why I
          chose you as my director.

INT. HOME OF BUDD SCHULBERG - OFFICE - EVENING

Budd walks in carrying his briefcase, he sits down at his
desk and ponders.

There's a knock at the door, the door opens, and Geraldine
sticks her head in.

                    GERALDINE
          May I come in?

                    BUDD
          Sure.

Geraldine walks in and approaches Budd.

                    GERALDINE
          You ok?

                    BUDD
          Mixed feelings.

                    GERALDINE
          Did you tell them?

                    BUDD
          I told Harry.

                    GERALDINE
          How'd he take it?

                    BUDD
          Ah, he wasn't happy about it.

                    GERALDINE
          When are you going to tell the rest
          of the group?

                    BUDD
          Tomorrow.

                    GERALDINE
          Five years -- Five years of blood
          sweat and tears that you poured
          into that workshop.

                    BUDD
          It was worth it. I have no
          regrets.

Geraldine kneels down in front of Budd, taking both of his
hands, she gently kisses his palms. Budd takes his hand and
gently caresses Geraldine's face.

EXT. WATTS - 9807 BEACH STREET - BACKYARD - DAY

MUSIC CUE: "Somebody's Watching You" by Little Sister.

Alvin "Ojenke" Saxon Jr., holding a transistor radio pulls on
a marijuana joint, he passes it to Samuel "Leumas Sirrah"
Harris.

                    ALVIN SAXON JR.
          Somebody's watching you.
          Somebody's watching youoooh.

Samuel "Leumas Sirrah" Harris takes a pull from the joint.
Johnie Scott, a cup of liquor in his hand takes a sip.

Cup in his hand, David Moody is wearing a cool-looking loud printed shirt and bell-bottom pants...

                    SAMUEL
          Leumas, pass me the joint.

Samuel takes another pull from the joint and passes it to David.

                    DAVID MOODY
          Righteous.

David takes two quick pulls from the marijuana joint, inhaling...

                    DAVID MOODY (CONT'D)
          Here you go, Ed.

Blowing smoke out of his mouth, David holds the joint out to Darthard Perry alias Ed Riggs who is wearing a dashiki shirt and bell-bottom jeans.

                    DARTHARD PERRY
          Cool.

Darthard Perry looks at what's left of the joint.

                    DARTHARD PERRY (CONT'D)
          Damn, man, it's down to a roach.

Perry sucks on the marijuana roach when Budd walks out the backdoor.

END MUSIC CUE:

                    BUDD
          Hey, can you guys come in for a
          minute? I want to talk to you.

Perry tosses the marijuana roach on the ground and steps on it.

INT. WATTS - 103RD & BEACH STREET - LIVING ROOM - DAY

Sitting on chairs and a couch are Harry Dolan, Jimmie Sherman, Charles Johnson, Eric Priestley, Sonora McKeller, Harley Mims, and Fannie Carole Brown.

Budd walks in followed by Johnie Scott, Alvin "Ojenke" Saxon Jr., Samuel "Leumas Sirrah" Harris, David Moody, and Darthard Perry.

Budd stands in front of everyone...

> BUDD
> Everyone couldn't make it. Off
> course we couldn't fit everyone in
> this small house anyway. When the
> workshop first took root, there
> were only fourteen of us. We've
> grown to over one hundred. I had
> to turn some people away. We have
> exceeded all expectations. This is
> hard, I felt, I have an obligation,
> to tell you that I'm leaving. I'm
> moving to New York.

Loud gasps are heard, stunned and surprised looks, and mouths are agape.

> CHARLES
> What's gonna happen to the
> workshop?

> JIMMIE
> What are we supposed to do without
> you?

> BUDD
> Don't worry, Harry is in charge.
> The workshop will continue to
> operate.

> JOHNIE
> It won't be the same without you.

> BUDD
> I'll check in from time to time.
> Continue to express yourselves
> through writing. You are a source
> of pride in Watts, a symbol of
> hope. Share that with others,
> touch lives. That's all I wanted
> when I came to Watts, and I believe
> I've done it.

Darthard Perry stares at Budd as he drags on a Pall Mall cigarette.

INT. STUDIO WATTS - 103RD & GRANDEE AVENUE - EVENING

In front of a hip-looking sparse group of black people. On a small stage performing to the rhythm of bongos are Anthony Amde Hamilton, Otis O'Solomon, and Richard Dedeaux.

                    AMDE
          I looked at the moon so full and
          bright. And then at the fireplace
          with it's flickering light. And
          realize why this world will never
          be right. Then I threw another log
          on the fire.

                    OTIS O'SOLOMON
          Let it burnnnnn.

                    AMDE
          Inside these four walls I am a
          king. But beyond that door it
          doesn't mean a thing. I pay all my
          dues, till I have only a partial
          membership in world happiness. And
          my blood runs freely in Vietnam.
          So I threw another log on the fire.

          OTIS O'SOLOMON   RICHARD DEDEAUX
     Let it burnnnnn.   Whooshhhhh.

                    AMDE
          Why do you insist on keeping us
          caged. You know all that does is
          intensify rage. The word now is
          seize the time. And all power to
          the people!

                    OTIS O'SOLOMON
          Power to the people!

                    RICHARD DEDEAUX
          Amandla! Amandla!

                    AMDE
          Then I threw another log on the
          fire. -- Putting us in a cage was
          a mistake. All that did was
          intensify hate. Now shackled to
          our cages you expect us to wait.
          While you fool around on the moon.
          And from there look for another
          place to conquer. While I throw
          another log on the fire.

          OTIS O'SOLOMON   RICHARD DEDEAUX
     Let it burnnnn.   Whooshhhhh.

                    AMDE
          America you argue is just doing
          fine.
                    (MORE)

                    AMDE (CONT'D)
         These racial things however do take
         time. Well I'm tired of waiting
         and not getting mine.

                    RICHARD DEDEAUX
         Me too!

                    AMDE
         Except however in Vietnam. Where
         every dead black man is a credit to
         his race. Uh, as long as he
         remembers his place. So I threw
         another log on the fire.

         OTIS O'SOLOMON   RICHARD DEDEAUX
    Let it burnnnnn.   Whooshhhhh.

                    AMDE
         Quick to put pencil to paper can't
         wait. Must write must explain
         before it's too late. The flames
         are at their peaks now can't wait.
         Too many broken promises.

                    OTIS O'SOLOMON
         Too many.

                    AMDE
         Too many black babies asking why.

                    RICHARD DEDEAUX
         Too many.

                    AMDE
         Too many restless armies in the
         ghetto.

         OTIS O'SOLOMON   RICHARD DEDEAUX
    Too many.   Too many.

                    AMDE
         So I'll just throw another log on
         the fire.

         OTIS O'SOLOMON   RICHARD DEDEAUX
    Let it burnnnnn.   Whooshhhhh.

    Richard begins to croon...

                    RICHARD DEDEAUX (CONT'D)
         A man can walk proudly down in his
         streets. A man's not ashamed of
         what he believes. He knows how to
         laugh. He knows how to cry.
                    (MORE)

                    RICHARD DEDEAUX (CONT'D)
          He knows how to live. He's not
          afraid to die. What is a man.
          Tell me, tell me, tell me, tell me,
          Otis. What is a man.

As the bongos fade down the sparse group of black people
applaud.

As Amde, Otis, and Richard walk off stage there greeted by
Alvin "Ojenke" Saxon Jr.

                    ALVIN SAXON JR.
          That was righteous man.   Real
          righteous.

                    AMDE
          Thanks, brotha. Ay, what you doing
          down here? Don't tell me you ready
          to join us.

                    ALVIN SAXON JR.
          Maybe. Schulberg is leaving, he's
          moving to New York.

                    OTIS O'SOLOMON
          Wow. The workshop is folding up?

                    ALVIN SAXON JR.
          Nah, Nah, Harry is running things.

                    AMDE
          Damn, Harry, huh, sticking with the
          establishment.

                    RICHARD DEDEAUX
          So where does that leave you?

                    ALVIN SAXON JR.
          I'm gonna keep writing, doing
          poetry.

                    AMDE
          Ay, man, well there's always a
          place for you here.

I/E. WATTS - SOUL FOOD CAFÉ - MORNING

MUSIC CUE: "Superstition" by Stevie Wonder.

Out front a few colorful black men and women mill about.

Harry Dolan smoking a cigarette sits at a table that looks
like an unorganized desk, with paper documents strewn on top.

Darthard Perry alias Ed Riggs walks up, peering through the window he sees Harry. Perry taps on the window, getting Harry's attention who then waves him over.

Perry walks through the front door and heads over to Harry's table, he takes a seat.

END MUSIC CUE:

> HARRY DOLAN
> Hey, man, what's happening?

Perry looks astonished by the disarrayed paper documents that lay before him.

> DARTHARD PERRY
> What's all this?

Harry, with some paper documents in hand, shuffles through them.

> HARRY DOLAN
> I have to make sense of all this.
> Applications for grants, letters to
> potential donors. Budget sheets.

> DARTHARD PERRY
> Where we gonna sit our food?

> HARRY DOLAN
> Yeah.

Harry collects all the paper documents shoving them into a briefcase.

> HARRY DOLAN (CONT'D)
> Look, man, I need you to work
> closely with me on a project.

> DARTHARD PERRY
> Whatever you need.

> HARRY DOLAN
> The Douglass Foundation is
> financially insolvent. I need
> forty grand to keep the Douglass
> House and the Douglass Theater
> operational.

> DARTHARD PERRY
> Have you talked to Budd?

                    HARRY DOLAN
So far I've been able to manage
things. If I call Budd asking him
about money. That makes me look
incompetent.

                    DARTHARD PERRY
Sounds like you don't have too many
options.

                    HARRY DOLAN
I have an idea that I know will
work.

                    DARTHARD PERRY
What's that?

                    HARRY DOLAN
A fundraiser. I'll put on a
fundraiser at the theater.

                    DARTHARD PERRY
That's a great idea.

                    HARRY DOLAN
We contact our donors and sponsors,
inviting them to attend. That
should solve the problem.

                    DARTHARD PERRY
I'm with you brotha, all the way.

Perry gets up from the table.

                    HARRY DOLAN
Where are you going?

                    DARTHARD PERRY
I just realized I have something I
have to take care of.

                    HARRY DOLAN
Don't want to eat?

                    DARTHARD PERRY
Nah, I'm cool. I'll catch up with
you later.

                    HARRY DOLAN
OK.

Perry walks off.

INT. L.A. FEDERAL BUREAU OF INVESTIGATION - OFFICE - DAY

There is a bustle of activity as FBI Agents move about.

Sitting at his desk looking over files is Brandon Cleary.
Michael Quinn walks up holding two brown paper bags and two
bottled cokes.

                    MICHAEL QUINN
          Hard at work?

Brandon sets the files down on his desk.

                    BRANDON CLEARY
          Cheeseburgers?

                    MICHAEL QUINN
          Indeed.

Michael hands Brandon one of the brown paper bags and a Coke.
He then takes a seat at a desk opposite Brandon Cleary.

Michael opens his desk drawer and grabs a bottle opener
popping the top off of the Coke bottle. He tosses the bottle
opener onto Brandon's desk.

                    BRANDON CLEARY
          Ay, my cheeseburger has onions on
          it. I said hold the onions.

Michael bites into his burger, chewing...

                    MICHAEL QUINN
          That's the only way to eat it.

The phone on Brandon's desk rings, and he picks up the
receiver.

                    BRANDON CLEARY
          Cleary.

Brandon's facial expression becomes alert, and he gestures to
Michael.

                    BRANDON CLEARY (CONT'D)
          OK -- We can't let that happen.
          Hell, I don't know, do whatever's
          necessary. Just don't let him pull
          it off.

Brandon hangs up the phone.

                    BRANDON CLEARY (CONT'D)
          That was Othello. Dolan's
          organizing a fundraiser to save the
          theater and the workshop.

                    MICHAEL QUINN
          So what's next?

                    BRANDON CLEARY
          I'm not sure. We'll see how he
          handles it.

INT. WATTS - HOUSE - ROOM - DAY

Looking dejected, Darthard Perry sits on the edge of the bed
holding a phone receiver in his hand, he hangs it up.

A two-year-old toddler wearing a t-shirt and diapers walks up
to Perry holding a toy.

                    DARTHARD PERRY
               Hey, baby, come here.

Perry embraces the toddler, and just then the Negro woman
walks in.

                    NEGRO WOMAN
          Come here, baby.

The Negro woman picks up the toddler.

                    NEGRO WOMAN (CONT'D)
          Darthard, the baby needs some more
          diapers.

                    DARTHARD PERRY
          You ain't potty-trained this child
          yet? The child is almost three
          years old.

Perry gets up from the bed and begins to walk away.

                    NEGRO WOMAN
          Where are you going?

                    DARTHARD PERRY
          I have some business to take care
          of.

                    NEGRO WOMAN
          Make sure you bring back some
          diapers.

                    DARTHARD PERRY
          Yeah.

EXT. WATTS - 1690 EAST 103RD - EVENING

On the large marquee that sits adjacent to the parking lot,
it reads *Douglass Watts Writers Theater Harry Dolan Presents
Douglass House Fundraiser*.

INT. WATTS - 1690 EAST 103RD - STAGE - EVENING

Dressed in a sport coat, business shirt, and slacks, Johnie
Scott stands at the microphone.

                    JOHNIE
               (reciting)
          ...And talk on telephones of the
          danger, and their children, and the
          nightmare that has descended and
          how hopelessness, helplessness is
          their. Young one's due. The man
          named fear has inherited half an
          acre, and is angry. -- Thank you.

Johnie walks off the stage to a round of applause.

Harry Dolan dressed in a suit walks up to the microphone.

                    HARRY DOLAN
          I want to thank everyone for coming
          out. This event was designed to
          raise awareness and donations for
          the Douglass Foundation. As many
          of you know...

INT. WATTS - 1690 EAST 103RD - CONTROL ROOM - CONTINUOUS

Sitting at the audio tape recorder, Darthard Perry dressed in
a suit with headphones on watches Harry Dolan through the
plexiglass.

As Darthard Perry operates the audio mixing board he hears
Harry Dolan's voice through the headphones.

                    HARRY DOLAN (V.O.)
          ...The Douglass House has been a
          beacon of pride and achievement for
          Watts. This theater is a haven and
          provides a resource for the
          talented voices of Watts...

INT. WATTS - 1690 EAST 103RD - STAGE - CONTINUOUS

Harry, on stage, addresses the audience.

                    HARRY DOLAN
          ...So I want to thank each and
          every one of you for your financial
          contributions. Those that have
          volunteered time. Cuz there is no
          Douglass House or theater without
          you. Thank you and goodnight.

The audience gives Harry a nice round of applause.

INT. WATTS - 103RD & BEACH STREET - LIVING ROOM - NEXT DAY

Johnie and Darthard are sitting on the couch when Harry walks
in.

                    JOHNIE
          We were just talking about you.

                    DARTHARD PERRY
          The fundraiser turned out nice.

                    HARRY DOLAN
          Yeah, it did. I was a little
          worried, but we hit our mark to
          keep things running.

                    JOHNIE
          Budd would be proud of you. You
          should call him and let him know
          how things went.

                    HARRY DOLAN
          Yeah, you're right. I'll call him.

                    DARTHARD PERRY
          So what's next?

                    HARRY DOLAN
          We have a couple of plays to
          produce. Some of the writers have
          lectures, speaking engagements.
          I'm lining up some paid gigs for
          the group.

                    JOHNIE
          You know I'm finishing up at
          Stanford, leaving with a degree, a
          B.A. in creative writing.

> HARRY DOLAN
> Go ahead then brotha.

> DARTHARD PERRY
> I'm getting my A.A. from L.A.C.C.,
> in communications.

> HARRY DOLAN
> See, that's what I'm talking about.
> There are so many success stories
> that have come out of the Watts
> Writers Workshop. We owe it all to
> Budd.

EXT. WATTS - 1690 EAST 103RD - NIGHT

A vague shadowy figure carrying a gas can and crowbar
approaches the back door entrance.

The vague shadowy figure jams the crowbar into the lock of
the backdoor and pry's it open.

INT. WATTS - 1690 EAST 103RD - THEATER - CONTINUOUS

The vague shadowy figure carrying the gas can begins
splashing gasoline all over the seats and on the stage.

INT. WATTS - 1690 EAST 103RD - CONTROL ROOM - CONTINUOUS

The vague shadowy figure walks in with the gas can and
splashes gasoline all over the video and audio recording
equipment.

INT. WATTS - 1690 EAST 103RD - THEATER - CONTINUOUS

The vague shadowy figure walks up to the stage, pausing to
take one last look. The vague shadowy figure strikes a flare
and tosses it onto the gasoline-soaked stage, POOF! The
stage is set ablaze.

The vague shadowy figure takes off running and disappears out
of sight.

INT. NEW YORK - HOUSE - OFFICE - DAY

The sound of a typewriter is heard...

On the wall are framed *posters* for the films *On the
Waterfront*, *The Harder They Fall*, and *A Face in the Crowd*.

Noticeably standing out on a mantle is an *Academy Award Statue.*

Seated at his desk wearing glasses typing away is Budd Schulberg. A phone on the desk rings, Budd pauses from typing and picks up the receiver.

                    BUDD
          Hello.

The voice of Harry Dolan is on the other end he sounds alarmed.

                    HARRY DOLAN (V.O.)
          Budd, it's me, Harry.

From Budd's facial expression, he senses something is wrong.

                    BUDD
          Harry, are you ok?

                    HARRY DOLAN (V.O.)
          No, I'm not. It's the theater,
          it's been burnt down.

                    BUDD
          What!

                    HARRY DOLAN (V.O.)
          You need to come back to Watts as
          soon as possible.

Budd looks completely stunned, he's speechless.

                    HARRY DOLAN (V.O.)
          Budd -- Budd, you hear me? Budd,
          are you there? Budd, Budd...

Budd shocked look, slowly hangs up the phone.

INT. SOUTH LOS ANGELES BAR - AFTERNOON

The hand of a black person slips a coin into a jukebox.

MUSIC CUE: "Why Can't We Live Together" by Timmy Thomas.

Brothers and sisters sporting afros dashiki shirts, bell bottom pants, hot pants, miniskirts, and Go-Go Boots party on the dance floor.

Darthard Perry wearing a dashiki shirt and smoking a Pall Mall cigarette sits alone at a table.

A waitress walks over to Perry and sets a glass of dark liquor on the table.

                    DARTHARD PERRY
          Thank you.

Perry takes a sip from the glass and drags on the cigarette, he looks quite comfortable.

Through the front door, a white man wearing flip-flops, jeans, and a tie-dye shirt walks in, it's FBI Special Agent Will Heaton.

Will looks around and spots Darthard Perry, they catch eye contact and Perry waves Will over to his table.

Will strolls over and takes a seat at Perry's table.

                    DARTHARD PERRY (CONT'D)
          You made it.

                    WILL HEATON
               (jest)
          You thought I would leave you
          hanging?

                    DARTHARD PERRY
          You wanna drink?

                    WILL HEATON
          Nah, no thanks.

Will looks around at all the black people. The atmosphere is hip, cool, and slick.

                    WILL HEATON (CONT'D)
          Man, your people have a certain
          style that's all their own. The
          music, fashion, culture.

                    DARTHARD PERRY
          That's what makes black people
          naturally cool.

                    WILL HEATON
          Black American culture has always
          been one of America's greatest
          exports. It has actually done
          important labor in terms of
          connecting global communities, both
          in terms of the interests of the
          United States and just people
          across the globe.

                    DARTHARD PERRY
          No, shit. You gonna lecture me
          about my people?

                    WILL HEATON
          We have to know something about the
          people we infiltrate.

                    DARTHARD PERRY
          Yeah, right. You got something for
          me?

Will discreetly slides an envelope to Darthard Perry who
nonchalantly takes the envelope.

On the envelope is a name, it reads, *Othello*. Perry peeks
inside the envelope and it's stuffed full of cash.

                    WILL HEATON
          You did a good job. Don't try to
          go anywhere, cuz we know how to
          find you. I'd love to stay here
          and party with your peeps, but I
          have other business.

Perry drags on the Pall Mall cigarette, blowing smoke from
his mouth.

                    DARTHARD PERRY
          Yeah.

Will gets up from the table and walks out the front door.

END MUSIC CUE:

I/E. WATTS - 1690 EAST 103RD - THEATER - DAY

Budd with a solemn look on his face, stares at the burnt-out
remains of the building.

As if taking a tour Budd walks through and steps over the
charred skeletal debris of what has been reduced to charcoal.

As Budd surveys the devastation, he ponders to himself...

                    BUDD (V.O.)
          A theater that was resurrected from
          ashes has once again been reduced
          to ashes.

In a daze, Budd continues to walk amongst the cinders and slag.

FADE OUT.

Roll Credits.

As the credits roll, we see actual footage of members from the Watts Writers Workshop -- Johnie Scott, Samuel "Leumas Sirrah" Harris, Alvin "Ojenke" Saxon Jr., Eric Priestley, Anthony Amde Hamilton, Quincy Troupe, Darthard Perry, and Budd Schulberg.

The End.